IRENE ROZDOBUDKO

The Lost Button

Glagoslav Publications

The Lost Button
By Irene Rozdobudko

First published in Ukrainian as "Гудзик"

Translated by Michael M. Naydan
and Olha Tytarenko

Cover Art by Janice Lucier

© Irene Rozdobudko 2005

© 2012, Glagoslav Publications, United Kingdom

Glagoslav Publications Ltd
88-90 Hatton Garden
EC1N 8PN London
United Kingdom

www.glagoslav.com

ISBN: 978-1-909156-04-3

Contents

ACKNOWLEDGEMENTS

An excerpt from *The Lost Button* was first published in the November-December 2011 issue of World Literature Today. First and foremost, I have a great debt of gratitude to the author Irene Rozdobudko for being so kind and helpful over the course of this translation of her novel. I am especially grateful to Svitlana Barnes for her kind assistance with proofreading, editing, and sharing her expertise on the manuscript at various stages of the translation, as well as for her support in the publication process. It has been fantastic for me to work with Olha Tytarenko on this project. Her expertise and fine work as co-translator have been invaluable.

A NOTE ON IRENE ROZDOBUDKO

Journalist, poet, translator, and novelist Irene Rozdobudko was born in 1962 in Donetsk in the Eastern and mostly Russian-speaking part of Ukraine. She completed her education as a journalist at Taras Shevchenko Kyiv National University. One should note that journalists in Ukraine take a considerable number of classes in literature as part of their curriculum. She worked first at a journalist in Donetsk after completing her studies and moved to Kyiv in 1988 where she took a position at the newspaper Rodoslav, as a copy editor of the scholarly and literary journal Suchasnist, as a reviewer for channels 1 and 3 of the National Ukrainian Radio Company, as a reviewer for the newspaper The Ukrainian News, as Deputy Editor of the glossy magazine Natali, as the editor-in-chief of the journal Caravan of History: Ukraine, and as a journalist for the magazine The Academy. She turned to writing prose fiction in her late thirties. Her first book, a detective novel, *A Trap for the Firebird* (2000), was initially published under the title *The Corpses* and republished later under its original title in 2007. It received second place in the national Coronation of the Word competition in Ukraine and was an immediate popular success. This launched her amazingly productive career as a fiction writer. That was followed by a flurry of publishing activity over the next twelve years, including the novels *He: The Morning Cleaning Man* (2005), *The Lost Button* (2005), *Twelve, or the Upbringing of a Woman in Conditions Not Suitable for Life* (2006), *Withered Flowers Get Tossed Out* (2006), *The Last Diamond of Milady* (2006), *Pascal's Amulet* (2007), *The Lives of Prominent Children* (2007), *When Dolls Come to Life* (2007), *Olenium* (2007), *Escort to Death* (2007), *Reformulation* (2007), *Two Minutes of Truth* (2008), *Everything I Wanted Today* (2008), *Playing with Beads* (2009), *Crossing the Darkness* (2010), *I Know That You Know that I Know* (2011), and *If* (2012). Her recent book *Travels without Sense and Moralizing* (2011) returns to her roots as a journalist and is a hybrid work in the style of New Journalism. Ms. Rozdobudko is a master of the detective novel and psychological thriller. She is one of the most popular writers in Ukraine today and writes in a lively, engaging style that makes her works accessible to a wide reading audience. She has also published two books of poetry in Russian, and several of her novels have been translated into Russian. The novel *The Lost Button* is appearing here in its entirety in English translation for the first time. A taut psychological thriller that keeps the reader transfixed, it received first place in the Coronation of the Word competition in 2005 and subsequently was made into a feature film.

The Lost Button begins with the story of a young student scriptwriter's encounter with a mysterious femme fatale actress by the name of Liza at a vacation resort in the Carpathian Mountains in Soviet Ukraine in the 1970s. Unable to let go of his love after getting lost with her during a storm in the woods for one beautiful and memorable night, the young man's fascination with the actress becomes an obsession for him after the end of their brief liaison. It nearly leads to his destruction. She coolly rebuffs him when fate places him in her class as one of her students, but he does meet her again many years later, at a point in time when he is a successful screenwriter and she has a grown daughter. The novel is unique in the way that with palpable psychological tension it traces the story over three decades of three intertwined fates from the diaristic perspective of each character at different stages of their lives.

The liner notes to the original edition of the novel put it aptly: "…great happiness or great tragedy can begin from the smallest detail, from a button, that is so easy to lose, but which you can search for your entire life… *The Lost Button* is a novel about love, devotion, and betrayal. It is about not looking back, but always valuing what you have – now and forever."

-- Michael M. Naydan

Irene Rozdobudko

The last day of August 2005

...I don't even remember coming home without being slightly tipsy. And probably not just slightly... Since yesterday I felt like someone had sewn a firecracker under my shoulder blade and that I'd just die if I looked at a glass of vodka or cognac. I had no way of quelling my anxiety. I had somehow to drag things out to the end of the workday. On the other hand, I wanted it to last forever. I was afraid to go home. I was afraid to sit at the computer. That's why after two not very onerous lectures in the Institute of Cinematography I went back to my office. I didn't have anything to do there. I could have even worked at home, thinking up endless scenes for advertising videos, but as I already noticed, I was afraid to go home. So I just sat for a while in my office, putting my feet on the desk, and from time to time obliging our office manager Tetyana Mykolaivna to bring me the strongest cup of coffee she could make. I looked out through the window. My stare was so sharp and focused that I saw the tiniest interlacing and furrows on the bark of an old tree that was growing on the other side of the street. I didn't tear my gaze away from those furrows, stuffed with gray cobwebs, and they reminded me of the deep furrows of an old man's face.

Summer was coming to a close. The year was racing to an end. I don't know about other people, but the year ends with the last day of August for me. Maybe because everything in my life seemed to begin in the fall....

I made every effort to turn off my brain, not to get lost in thought. But mentally I had already been in my apartment a hundred times and made several of my customary movements: I opened the door, took off my sport coat, sat down at the computer, settled myself into a deep black armchair, and clicked the mouse.

Why in truth am I so afraid of doing all this? What's stopping me right now from taking my feet off the table, snatching up my briefcase, jumping into the street, sitting behind the wheel and in about ten minutes firmly pushing open the door of my own apartment? What kind of weights had been strapped to my feet? In time I understood that these "weights" were the fear of not finding anything on the monitor screen. NOTHING at all.

But with considerable fear I thought about a little yellow email icon folder lighting up in the corner of the screen.

And I didn't know what was better: that nothing or the icon folder....

Close to eight o'clock Tetyana Mykolaivna began to cough pathetically at my door. And then, opening it slightly, asked:

"More coffee?"

I knew it was time to go. I stepped out into the street and at first didn't go in the direction of my favorite restaurant, Suok,[1] though I could have... But the urge overwhelmed me on the street, I felt its fever and barely came rushing to my building entryway. Then I was afraid the elevator would suddenly get stuck and I would have to be bored stiff in it for a few endlessly long hours, wondering whether the icon folder was there?...

Thank God that didn't happen, and I tore into the apartment while I was still in motion taking off my sport coat, tossing my shoes and tie every which way. I fell into my black armchair, having more than enough of a fiery look on my face. It would have been interesting what my students who have gotten used to my complete "buttoned down" straight-laced nature would have said?

I held my breath....

...At that time the weather was almost the same. Watermelons rested on the balcony.

---

1 Suok is the name of a character in Yuri Olesha's fairytale "Three Fat Men." She is a girl who takes the place of a mechanical doll for a boy.

Right now there's a thick layer of street dust.

I clicked the button. In the corner a little yellow folder appeared. Everything was the way I had imagined it – and I didn't believe it myself. Really? I clicked it with the mouse. Then I shut my eyes and opened it up.

"I died on the 25th of September 1997…," the first line flashed on the blue background of the monitor.

I shut my eyes again. The cold and darkness shackled me….

PART ONE
DENYS

1.

It happened at the end of August 1977… I had just turned eighteen then. I was dreaming about fame. And I knew it would come. It wasn't about some kind of temporary ascent onto a pedestal in the small space where I lived then. It wasn't about the applause of the audience that forgets you the next day. No. I sensed that some kind of mission was there for me, the mystery of which I needed to solve. But for the time being it was being generated somewhere deep inside me, as though beans had germinated in a damp cheesecloth – we did that kind of experiment in biology classes in school. All thirty-five students grew beans on their window sills, and after a few weeks brought the results to school. I remember well that my sprout was larger than the other ones. It happened a long time ago in the sixth grade. But after my experiments, I understood what and how things develop inside me. And I patiently waited. So patiently that I tried not to call unnecessary attention to myself – while I couldn't care less. For the time being.

I finished school, quite easily got into the scriptwriting program of the Department of Film (my exam film script turned out to be better than the opuses of already experienced and much older prospective students, and they kept it for a long time in the department as a particularly successful sample). After learning the admission test results, I went for a small vacation to the mountains, to a tourist hostel at the foothills of the Carpathian Mountains. In fact, this was a cinematographer's hostel to which all my future classmates went – an announcement about unused student passes hung in the hall of the Institute. We didn't know each other well yet. We were united by the common spirit of the recent exams, during which we all crowded around jovially by the doors of the classrooms, clamorously saluting each lucky individual.

All this was behind us. We arrived at the tourist hostel little by little, without making any arrangements beforehand with each other, and ardently reveled at each familiar face. They put us up in small wooden buildings, and we immediately began to explore the territory, finding out where the dining room, swimming pool, and movie hall were along with the closest *Silpo* general store, where you could buy the cheapest port wine.[2]

We felt we were grown up and experienced. We tried to communicate with each other in a loosey-goosey way and uttered the names of our idols like good buddies. We gave each other a Western name, that's why I was immediately christened "Dan." My roommate, accordingly, was called Max.

Dan and Max – two cool guys, the future geniuses quickly ran over to the *Silpo* general store and loaded up on several bottles of strong "ink." We drank like fish since our grade school days and… like juveniles – nothing more expensive than cheap port wine. To be truthful, a little later I was sorry I had gone there....

The mountains turned deep blue in the distance, and it seems they were glimmering, enveloped by the torn white silk of an evening veil. And I was forced to sit on a hard bed, chugging the port wine and listening to the chitchat of my acquaintances. When we all started to get sick (no one, of course, complained and we tried our best to maintain our dignity), we began to take our turns going out "for a

2 "777" wine. An inexpensive high alcohol context (18%) wine made in the former USSR and now in Russia and Ukraine.

breath of fresh air." I finally managed to tear myself away from the smoky room and, already no longer in a hurry, to stroll along the grounds of the camp.

This was quite a quiet little spot. Or else it appeared that way at the end of the summer. Behind the curtains of the cottages a dusky light shimmered, vacationers were sitting in spots on the verandas, from an open "green" movie hall the sound of the music from a film echoed. It seems like it was the movie *Yesenia*.[3] Altogether it was disorder and havoc. Just beyond an old-fashioned fence in pseudo-baroque style, the shaggy black forest murmured alluringly, and from it a powerful wave of freshness and anxiety rolled onto me. It was already quite dark. Simple sculptures of girls with oars and other body builders snowily-whitely shone on both sides of the alleys like ghosts. Almost all the benches were "toothless," and all the lamps "blind." I walked up to the end of the alley, sat down on a bench, and pulled out my cigarettes from my pocket. And nearly right away I noticed the flash of a red glow across from me… If I had not been drunk then, and if, like the wine, the drunken feeling of the euphoria of an entry into a new life had not been playing inside me – nothing would have happened and would not have caused a chain of events that would pursue me my entire life.

But I was drunk. That's why I saw *something*… A silhouette, etched by the light of the moon resembling an incorporeal, empty outline in the total darkness. A woman was smoking a cigarette in a long mouthpiece. She slowly raised the small red glow to her invisible lips, inhaled, and for an instant the silvery smoke filled her entire outline, as though it were sketching her body from the inside.

And then, with the last small cloud of smoke, it, this body, once again melted into the darkness.

Jeez!

---

3   A Mexican melodramatic film from 1974 that was very popular as a rental video in Soviet times. See: http://www.videoguide.ru/card_film.asp?idFilm=17763.

I strained my eyes and comically waved my hand before my nose, chasing away the apparition.

"What, you got scared?"

The voice was husky, but so sensuous that I got goose bumps over my entire body, as though the woman had uttered something obscene (even later I couldn't get used to her voice: whatever she talked about – the weather, books, movies, food – everything sounded sweetly-obscene, like candor).

"Well no… I'm fine…," I mumbled.

However, the damp night and the appearance of the mountain summits that were blackening in the distance, and this little red light, and the wind – so saturated and fresh – sobered me up. I tried to get a good look at the woman who was sitting across from me. No use. Maybe at that moment I was already completely blinded by her. A similar thing happens, for example, with mothers who aren't able to honestly judge the beauty of their own child, or with an artist, for whom the most recent canvas seems to be a work of genius.

"Are you staying at this resort house?"

I couldn't have thought up anything more idiotic to say! It's the same as if you were to ask a passenger after the plane takes off, "Are you also flying in this plane?" But I itched to hear that voice again.

"Do you like it here?" I continued.

The glow flashed even brighter (she took a drag) and slid down (she lowered her hand).

"Do you know where I like it?" I heard (goose bumps! goose bumps!) after quite a long pause. "There."

The tiny glow of her cigarette flicked in the direction of the forest.

"I haven't been there yet…," I said. "I arrived just today…."

"Strange!" The fire in an instant flew into a bush and went out. "Let's go! There's a hole here in the fence…."

By the rustle of her clothing I understood that she had gotten up and took a step in my direction.

"Give me your hand!"

I stretched into the darkness and stumbled on a chilly palm. I got goose bumps again. Her hand was hearty, not soft.

"E-eh, you're completely drunk!" She started to laugh.

I got up, trying to keep steady. We were the same height. I was able to discern something more or less definite: an elongated figure, a dark, possibly black shawl that covered her shoulders… But nothing more. And I also could smell her scent.

Back then I still didn't know the scent of expensive perfumes – they got them from under their skirt on the sly, girls I knew for the most part used the overwhelming Scheherazade or the highly concentrated Lily of the Valley brands. And here suddenly a wave of a fragrant aroma – bitter and dizzying – wafted in on me. Involuntarily I clenched my teeth and pressed her hand more tightly. Giving in to her will, I swiftly moved toward a dead end where the fence stopped. There really was a big black hole in it, which I didn't notice right away. Without letting go of her hand, walking after her, I bent my head down sharply, and we ended up on the other side of the tourist hostel on a wide plain that was overgrown with tall grass. We walked, buried in it up to our knees. Again I tried to look over the woman who had commandingly led me by the hand like a little boy. Her long black shawl covered her from head to toe, the length of her hair was also unclear to me – it flowed with her shawl and in full sight was just as black and long. Not even once did she turn back toward me. It seemed she was completely indifferent to whomever she was dragging behind her.

I strove not to fall and not to lag behind, so I began to look beneath my feet more often, and the wild vegetation reminded me of the sea that rolls powerful, fragrant waves and just about drags you to a depth, from which you can't swim away.

My head was topsy-turvy. The night, a thin crescent of the moon above clouds, mountains, goose bumps all over my body, intoxication, this unknown woman... Everything seemed to be phantasmagoric. I cherished these kinds of adventures. I couldn't imagine what would happen further! Maybe wild sex in a clearing in the forest? Who was this woman? Why and where was she taking me? How old was she, what does she look like? What does she want? We walked up to the slope of the mountain covered in trees that rose above the clearing like columns next to the entrance of a pagan temple. The gloom again swallowed her, and from the forest the particular thick scent of resin wafted. The woman led me beyond the fence of the first stand of large pine trees, from which the forest began, and leaned up with her back against one of the trees.

"Wonderful, isn't it?"

I barely caught my breath and looked around. Really, it was wonderful! It was as if we had ended up in the bowels of some great living organism, some fairytale fish. The trees were its twisted muscles, it breathed through the treetops, and somewhere inside, in the depth, slowly, its heart beat. I even could hear this rhythmic, uneasy sound.

"It's alive. Do you sense it? During the day it's all not quite like this...."

She clicked her cigarette lighter and for an instant I saw the semicircle of her cheek and the flash of her black pupil. Then once again the red glow began to dance in front of me.

"What's your name?" I asked, persistently thinking how this strange adventure might end.

"What's the difference? Especially now...."

The red glow traced an arc and disappeared. And again I sensed that I had been taken by the hand and dragged somewhere higher. We walked so quickly, as though we were escaping after being chased. I heard her intermittent breathing. At a certain moment things got uncomfortable for me. Branches of trees that I didn't manage to brush aside from time to time smacked me in the face.

Finally, we made our way even higher and stopped. Everything repeated – her merging with the tree, the red glow.

This time with wonder I looked below: we had come out of the maw of the beast, and in the distance the outlines of the closest village were being painted by vague little lights, intersected by the golden line of the river. From here, the thick tops of trees that grew below seemed like clustered storm clouds, along which you could walk as though on dry land. I completely came to my senses and breathed avariciously, enjoying the strange taste of the air, which I was able to appreciate just now. Together with this air, rapture filled me. How good it was that I had torn myself away from the stifling room, stumbled upon this woman, and she led me on such a wonderful stroll! I understood that two weeks of my vacation would be wonderful. I turned back, I wanted to thank her….

The glow disappeared. I walked up to the tree where she had just been standing. I had even touched it with my palm. No one there!

"Halloo," I hailed quietly, "where are you?"

My voice echoed unusually in the darkness. Somewhere not far away a night bird began to flap its wings. I walked around each tree, each bush. A mad thought entered my brain that somewhere she had spread out her shawl, had lain on it and was waiting, so that I'd stumble on her body more quickly.

Then I became angry: what kind of idiotic prank was this?! Then I began to worry whether I could find the way back. And then a little later I inopportunely recalled that this place was swarming with legends about mermaids, *niavka* river nymphs, *mavka* forest nymphs, *molfar* wizards, and witches….

It was unpleasant enough to go down the mountain myself. The entire time I listened attentively to try to hear the sound of her footsteps nearby. But the forest only breathed deeply and grabbed at me with its stiff fingers. I even fell twice.

Coming out onto a flat clearing, I took a breath and again looked around at the forest. It seemed to me that up above once again the red little glow of her cigarette was breathing. It was observing me like an eye. And maybe, it was laughing....

2.

Confused and dirty I returned to my room where my roommate was already snoring loudly. I fell onto the bed on top of the covers. I took my clothes off and pulled the covers over myself just before dawn when clouds were already turning pink outside the window. I quickly glanced at the mountain. Now it seemed to be brown, as though it were covered in multi-colored patches. We were late for breakfast. I took a long time to clean off my slacks. Max wasn't able to come to his senses after yesterday's drinking bout.

"Where'd you go?" He asked.

"Well, I decided to go for a walk," I waved my hand timidly. I didn't feel like telling anyone at all about my evening adventure on the mountain. I decided to look for last night's companion today. It's true I remembered very little: dark hair, a shawl that blazed behind her shoulders, the outline of a dark-complexioned cheek in the flash of a lighter, a tiny red glow... But there was also the scent – the special scent of her perfume.

In the dining hall I furtively looked over those who were there. Half of the vacationers had already left, each one doing his or her thing – some made their way to the forest for mushrooms, others went to take in the local museums and views. She, in all likelihood, also had already had breakfast and left.

"Who's still here from our group?" I asked Max.

"You already saw everyone!" He was surprised.

"I have in mind in general – from among the film students?" I explained. For some reason, I thought she might be a student from the acting department. Max named several more or less well-known names for me. But all this was not right. We lazily picked at our plates: vermicelli with a moldy sour gherkin, cottage cheese with crème fraîche… The half-empty dining hall that reeked of lime and its blue walls didn't rouse our appetite. Several people were sitting at two neighboring tables. I recognized one gray-haired documentary filmmaker in a tattered jeans jacket (how we used to dream back then of having a foreign rag like that!). He was with his daughter and wife. Three girls were sitting a bit further away. They were exchanging remarks loudly, chortling, and casting a glance first at Max and me, then in the direction of the dour documentary filmmaker. One of the women was smoking. She was quite stout with short hair.

"It looks like we're going to die of boredom here!" Max noted. Though you could go on a three-day trek to the mountains. I saw an ad on a notice board. What do you think about that?"

"I'm not sure yet…."

We somehow sloughed through the vermicelli, and with a certain amount of satisfaction drank up two glasses of cold kefir and stepped out into the sun. I still didn't know Max well enough and I felt like breaking away to go for a walk alone.

"Well, where are you going?" I asked involuntarily.

"I'll take a little snooze," he answered. "And you?"

"I'll go for a walk."

In the morning the grounds of the tourist camp had a completely uninviting look. The sculptures were awful and the gazebos broken. Just unclipped bushes, the tall trees on both sides of alleys and flowerbeds in various-colored caps of roses were natural and weren't annoying. Despite it all I liked this desolation. I went over to the swimming pool. Several people were walking near it, but no one dared to dive into the greenish water that was covered in duckweed. Most likely it was rainwater and had stood in this concrete trough the entire summer. Along the dark, opaque surface, maple leaves glided along like little boats. I saw her right away. I was worried for no reason that I wouldn't recognize her! She was lying on a striped towel and reading a book. Her hair was really dark and thick – it was gathered into a long ponytail. She was in an open tank suit. Nothing in common with yesterday's nocturnal image of her. And I was sure it was her. I sat down on the opposite end of the swimming pool and began to look her over. To no avail! Again I felt a strange blurriness in my eye – as much as I stared, I couldn't gather a complete image of her. It fell apart like children's blocks. Did she have a nice figure? I contemplated her delicately pink heels that shone in the sun. They seemed like the apples of paradise. Maybe she was just like everyone else. But certainly the meaning of human relations consists of the fact that at some moment "one of everyone" seemingly ends up at the intersection of heavenly rays and becomes the first, the only one of everyone… I saw her in just such a perspective – as though she were an airplane led by two spotlights. The rest of space became dark and uninteresting for me. It made no sense to stare at her so intently anymore. I walked over to her. I made room for myself next to her on the grass and immediately sensed that tart, foreign aroma, except it was much weaker and softer in the morning. She tore her gaze away from the book and looked in my direction. I was not sure if she recognized me, but I understood that the usual manner of getting acquainted won't work here. Should I ask her what she's reading or whether she believes in love at first sight? No, too trite… Quote her a few lines from Baudelaire? Makes no sense… Talk about the weather? No way….

"Don't get worked up," she suddenly said to me. "My name is Liza.[4] Didn't you want to know that?"

Her voice bared me completely! She turned on her side, propped her chin on her hand, and looked me right in the eyes. The sun shone on her swarthy shoulder, blinding me.

"Where did you disappear?" I asked.

"In general I like to disappear," she answered and again concentrated on the book. But I already couldn't live without her voice!

"Maybe we can climb up the mountain?" I suggested. "Or take a trip to town to sit for a bit in a café?"

"Don't think so. I have enough cafes at home. And it's too hot on the mountain right now."

I sat next to her till lunchtime. My friends shouted for me to come to the volleyball court a hundred times, then to the woods, some of the "old-timers" said "hello" to her. From time to time we exchanged a few pleasantries. In general, nothing special. But she comported herself in a regal way. When she tired of my presence, she said:

"That's it, enough. Go to your friends. Why are you sitting here languishing next to me?"

"Can we see each other in the evening?" I asked her hopefully.

"Where can we escape to from here…."

She didn't understand me! If I were making a movie, with contentment I'd cut out a couple or three days from this tape to move to the main action right away. I already understood that I'll be attempting to be worthy of her attention, that we definitely will go up the mountain again and that I'll try and give her a warm embrace. But what will she do? That wasn't in my script….

---

4   Pronounced "Leeza."

3.

"Do you know who you were watching over all morning?" Max asked after we met in the room before lunch.

I was embarrassed. I didn't feel like chit-chatting about her. That is – at all.

"That was Elyzaveta Tenetska!"

The name was familiar to me, but I couldn't remember where I had heard it.

"Really!" Max got more excited. "Remember last year's Film of the Year youth festival? She got first place for the short *Madness*!

That's it! Of course, since ninth grade I've being going to that all-night vigil, I gate-crashed it without any invitation with every truth and lie until after I got into prep courses, I finally got the proper admission ticket to go there without any problems. Back then it was tough: at the entrance they checked your pockets for bottles of alcohol (we used to bring port wine in thermoses). Additionally, you needed to have your Communist Youth League ticket with you.

The festival lasted from morning till midnight with short breaks for the jury's deliberation, during which the tired audience had the opportunity to eat dried sandwiches at the buffet counter of the Palace of Culture and to gulp "nourishing moisture" from our thermoses.

I really liked the movie. It even dazzled me. It was filmed very simply without pretense, without the least hint of any kind of ideology. This was strange, unusual. Discussion of it dragged on for two or three hours. But no one left until the members of the jury heated in debates announced their winners, and the representatives of the cultural sections of the regional committee, the *oblast* committee and the rest of the observers ingloriously abandoned the field of battle, calling out this assemblage "a bacchanalia on the bones of true art."

I could hardly retell the plot in detail. It was a short movie-novella about loneliness. The day of a woman – from morning till night – who aimlessly wanders through a big city. And the ending: an ambulance, people in blue gowns, broken arms, the despairing eyes of the heroine. As it turned out in the end, she had escaped from a psychiatric hospital. That's it… I couldn't understand how this kind of movie could have ended up at all in this Communist Youth League film festival. Later I often remembered it, but never identified this movie with the female name of the author, I didn't try to figure out who she was. And here now I was agitated, stupefied. Was this really her? These terra cotta colors, intentional scratches on the tape, this filming in the manner of "looking through a keyhole"… I was terrified. It didn't scare me that she was older and more talented – that all just aroused my imagination. I just sensed that a high wave was coming at me and that the most sensible thing to do would be to never get close to her. But I was too young for that kind of decision.

Though I did have a bit of experience in contacts with women. My father worked as the main engineer at one of the biggest factories in the city, I had money to play with. To "learn about life" my friends and I often used to sit in restaurants, played at the hippodrome, went hiking, and sometimes our adventures were quite dangerous. We, of course, couldn't get by without women. But for the time being didn't have any serious flames. Though I'm sure that I spoiled the impression for many of that feeling that's called "first love." I tried not to date a girl for more than a month, and most often – for just a week. I strove for everything, a lot and all at once. The feeling of firm relations brought me awful boredom. I never felt remorse a single time.

Truth be told, one instance forced me to give pause….

Then we – I and two of my older friends – were sitting in the Lisovy[5] Restaurant and were picking up "morsels" worthy for continuation of the banquet at Myshka's place.

---

5 Meaning "forest."

He was a guy from a well-to-do family, lived in a four-room apartment in the center of town, and was often left alone while his parents were observing the "decaying" capitalism of western countries.

My friends had already each selected a girl and waited for the VIE (vocal instrumental ensemble – as it was called back then) to tune their guitars in order to invite the girls to dance, and in due time – home. I, as always, was looking for *something*….

Overtly beautiful babes, who looked like a model, as you might say today, didn't attract me. I never liked big-eyed, long-legged blondes – it was the same, I thought, as sleeping with a blow-up doll. Though it was a lot easier to come to an understanding with those types. The objects of my attention usually didn't go to restaurants (though by those measures it cost a pretty kopeck).

"Well, what do you think?" My friends impatiently asked me.

I waved them off and gazed in every direction. And when I already had completely lost hope and tossed my glance at an over-ripened matron at a neighboring table, three girls entered the room.

"Everything's o'kay!" I reported, like a fisherman who finally "has a bite."

One of the girls was wearing a black dress. That struck me. In the summer, when everyone wears light colors, she dressed up like a raven, and with that really distinguished herself from the others. Besides that, she had natural hair of an unusual, bronze shade – downy, "with a sparkle." In a word, really nice hair….

I called over the waiter and asked him to take over a bottle of champagne to the girls. I liked to "play the officer gentleman" thing, and mainly to observe the expressions that similar actions effect, because women then weren't yet accustomed even to elementary things, not to mention "free cheese." So they, too, immediately bent their heads and began to whisper animatedly, darting their eyes along the room. At first they even wanted to return the bottle. The waiter explained something to them for a long time, and then (there, the riffraff!) nodded in the direction of our table. All three of them, as if by command, looked in our direction, and then just as sharply turned away, pretending to be indifferent. I tried to guess what they could have been talking about. First, they were deciding to which of the three the unexpected gift belonged (judging by the way the face of the bronze-haired one blazed up, her girlfriends were convincing her of that). Second, they were racking their brains over the question: what to do next… Third, they were debating over us and imagining who of the three of us has made this regal gesture. The dancing began. I placed an end to their doubts. I walked up and asked the red-haired girl to dance. Then we sat together at one table till the restaurant closed and generously paid for the girl's whims – chocolate, crab salad, a bottle of "Bear's Blood."[6] No one had any doubts that the evening would end at Myshka's apartment. The name of the girl in black was Sasha. But that name calamitously didn't fit her, and her nickname Shurochka sounded even more inane. Her dress, when I looked more closely, turned out to be homemade and cheap, her boots – children's school ones. She had just graduated from high school; her girlfriends worked at the sewing factory. Without taking into consideration the fact that these factory girls turned out to be livelier, "mine" tried not to lag behind them. Just after we arrived at Myshka's apartment, without hesitation, she ended up in bed with me. When I asked her later why – with wonderment Sasha darted back at me: "You treated us!" Ha! Like a respectable girl she made haste to settle accounts! I remember her the longest. And not only because her dress and red hair struck me (fog swallowed the rest of her image) – she was from some other world. And that frightened me. Back then I couldn't fathom that it exists! We got together several

---

6   A famous red wine from Hungary called Egri Bikaver in Hungarian.

times. But somehow half-heartedly: new impressions lured me, and she was too amorphous in her attitude to many things that captivated me – the latest premiere at the theater, a new collection of Yevtushenko poems, festivals of bard-poets.

Our relations ended as quickly as they began after one incident. We were walking along the street and looking at workers lifting up a giant banner with the photographs of members of the Politburo.

"There's a bunch of pigs," Sasha suddenly said, "and we're their feeding trough...."

I, the beloved son of the chief engineer of a famous factory, grew indignant – how could she say something like that?

"Of course... they carry things too far, but in general," I muttered, "you need to be a patriot of the country you live in...."

"All the patriots are doing time in prison!" She cut me off.

"What do you mean "doing time in prison?" I couldn't understand. "Criminals are doing time in prison."

"Aha, criminals," my red-haired girl couldn't restrain herself, "Brodsky, Stus, Solzhenitsyn...[7] All of them are criminals!"

"Well, let's presume, Brodsky went to prison for loafing," I wouldn't give in, though I sensed that something wasn't right. I couldn't say anything about the others.

"Aha," she said even more bitingly, "a poet needs to bust his guts!"

"Why, don't you think they should?"

Here she bit her little tongue, though her cheeks were blazing. Afterward when I returned home and analyzed that conversation, I decided that the girl had listened to unnecessary crap from her parents. And I got frightened.

---

7   The Russian poet Joseph Brodsky, the Ukrainian poet Vasyl Stus, and the Russian prose writer Alexander Sozhenitsyn. All three of them were imprisoned in the GULAG by the Soviet regime.

Theoretically I knew that there are people out there who are unhappy with the powers that be. But to encounter this through some little snot this way! Life to me seemed beautiful, and I didn't want disturbance, confusion and disorder to enter it. Everything talented, I thought, needs to overcome obstacles. Otherwise it's uninteresting! And she repeated like a parrot: "Freedom can't be divided into doses!" And I didn't understand what she had in mind. And did she really understand this with her nearly childlike intellect? Hardly. Most likely she was repeating words of grownups… Traitors and strikebreakers! Our dates ended. But later I was to remember Sasha more and more often. And I began to understand, WHAT she was saying and felt myself to be a complete piece of trash, an idiot and a wretch. Strange, but it was this girl whom I remembered when I watched *Madness*, that Elyzaveta Tenetska had filmed.

I remembered her right now. Perhaps because a feeling engulfed me now a bit similar to what I experienced back then, just this time it was stronger, sharper: I DIDN'T SEE my new acquaintance. I was indifferent to what she was like – her figure, the color of her eyes, legs, arms, hair, and finally – her age. The only thing that was important was: that she exists.

My roommate assured me that "Tenetska is super." But even if that were not so – all the same! She existed, like the sky, in which I had wandered, losing my balance and falling, not noticing anything beneath or above me….

4.

Later we often saw each other in the dining hall, in the movie hall, then near the swimming pool. She would invitingly nod her head to me and pass by. In a word, about five days of my film script could easily be thrown out. I looked for an opportunity. And finally I saw her name in a list of the instructor, who was gathering a group for a hike into the mountains. I rushed to get some money – a two-day trip cost about fifteen rubles – and then walked up to him.

"You're late," an older fellow in crumpled short pants said categorically. "The group's already set."

"But what's the difference? Can't you sign up one more person?"

"The instructions say – it's twelve!" He cut me off, "You can go next time. You've dragged your feet too long!"

"What kind of dumb instructions?" I didn't stop, "Don't you want to make some money?"

"Ha! This isn't your private shop, I'm here in service to the government. Twelve is the number that was designated there…," he pointed his finger up in the air.

"By God?" I tried to joke.

"Don't blaspheme, young man. Why should I be responsible for a larger number of people? If I hadn't been able to gather a full group – then by all means! So I don't need any additional problem. I won't get a bonus for you alone."

Then I instantly ran to the cottage and added another twenty to the fifteen rubles I had already offered.

"Will that be good?"

The old guy became more animated, got his list, and with a look of importance added my name to it.

"We're meeting tomorrow at six in the morning next to the dining hall. You'll get lunch like rations! Be sure you're not late!" He ordered harshly.

…The morning turned out to be chilly; it had the bitter taste of autumn that was approaching. This taste was particularly felt in the morning hours. I shaved, put on my tee-shirt and a clean sweater, rubbed my cheeks with Chypre cologne, and shoved into my knapsack a bottle of homemade red wine that I bought last evening from an older local lady.

What was I counting on? I don't know. Maybe, in the evening, when we put up our tents, I'll manage to take a stroll with her?...

And I stuffed into my pockets all the money I had, a box of matches, a knife, and a writing pad. I arrived at the dining hall first. I'd have another half hour to guess: would she appear? I already surmised that her actions might be unforeseen. After twelve of us had gathered, the instructor began to nervously look at his watch. She finally appeared at the end of the alley.

"Our star in our repertoire!" Someone commented.

Besides me and her, in the group there were two couples with teenage children – seven in total, two older ladies the age of Balzac, and a documentary filmmaker with his daughter. Deathly boredom! But I understood that I had no competitors, and she had no choice. That's why just as she approached I took her bag and threw it over my shoulder.

"Well, comrades," the instructor addressed us, "I'll lead you through the shortest path: so we don't have to walk around the entire territory, we'll go through the alley – there's a hole in the fence… This, of course, is inappropriate, but we aren't going to waste time!"

I quickly looked at Liza. She was smiling.

And we went along a path I knew well – through a meadow to the foot of the mountain.

"I don't know why I would need all this…," Liza said as though she were continuing a conversation, "I don't like communal activities. But it's so boring here…."

"You rejected having a good time. I invited you…," I answered, completely forgetting whether we switched to calling each other the informal "ty" instead of the formal "vy."[8]

She looked at me strangely:

---

8   Like the French "tu" and "vous."

"…and we'd talk about the movies?…."

Here I understood how I needed to talk with her. I understood it, but I couldn't utter a single word, like a foreigner, who was just beginning to learn a language.

"We could have just kept silent," I answered.

When the group began to ascend higher up the mountain, the conversations in our not well formed ranks quieted down, the women wheezed, the men, like true gentlemen, took their backpacks and panted even more vigorously. Everyone took off their sweaters. The sun slowly heated up the damp forest, and the night steamed out of it. We passed the spot where Liza previously had abandoned me. Again I felt anxiety. I understood that she could return and go just about any moment. But later it was already too late – we had gone up too far and came out onto a valley – a mountain pasture. The large glade was surrounded by wild cherry trees. The berries were red and tiny.

We halted by one of the trees. I bent over a branch and we nearly simultaneously bit off several berries with our lips… (*I already had fallen in love with her! I was fearful of glancing at her again – my eyes were irritated from doing that like from the flare of a flashlight, and even more, the fire of wild desire was burning me from within, I was covered in sweat, turned red, shaking like a leaf. And I hated myself for my lack of restraint*).

"Let them go to the devil!" Liza shouted suddenly in the direction of the twins that already has crossed the valley. "We're going in formation like pioneers. And there's such beauty everywhere…."

It was difficult to imagine anything better than this.

"Let's hide until they go!" I suggested.

She got lost in thought.

"Maybe we'll ruin their entire holiday. They'll search…."

"Then I suggest we just get lost. Accidentally. Doesn't that happen?"

"Aha. And in the morning in the local newspaper an article will appear entitled "An Incident in the Mountains"… In fact, you just enrolled at the institute. They can expel you! I have nothing to lose. They've already washed my films…."

"That means?" I didn't understand.

"Very simple: they take the film and put it into a chemical solution…."

"And they've washed *Madness* out?"

"Of course!" She smiled evilly. "Could it be any other way? This is like… Like a forced abortion in the eighth month…."

She took out a cigarette from a pack, slowly released a stream of smoke and looked at me with squinting eyes:

"You're handsome. Has anybody said that to you?"

Before I answered her, I subdued a pile of various emotions, and mainly deafness that for a moment overwhelmed me (my heart was rattling right in my head!).

"I don't remember…," I answered as indifferently as possible.

"Good, let's go further!" She ordered. "Otherwise, we'll really get lost."

But we had gotten lost all the same! After crossing the valley, we couldn't figure out in which direction the group had gone. My heart was singing. In order not to show my joy, I had to run and call out for a bit, but no one answered me.

"Does this look natural to you?" I asked.

"Completely. Maybe we should go back?"

"Why?!" I assume we'll catch up to them by evening. We'll follow the smoke of the campfires to find them.

So we walked on further again, climbing up, then going down into a valley, stopped, were quiet for a bit, enchanted by nature, we fell into the tall grass and drank water from a small mountain stream. The evening fell quickly, like a stone. In that time we were approaching yet another foot of a mountain. We had to run and shout again for a bit, looking for an encampment with tents. Mentally I prayed that no one would answer me. In fact, that's what happened.

"Now," Liza said, "we need to set up a campfire and stay here till morning. Maybe they'll find us on the way back."

"Are you afraid?" I asked her in trepidation.

"Who, me!?" She started to laugh. "The worst thing has already happened to me. Now there will be happening to me just… the beautiful. Is it bad here?"

Blue twilight that flowed out of the forest covered us in a thick wave. We stood in it up to our necks. And after a while unknown nocturnal scents and mysterious sounds, which you weren't able to sense in the morning, engulfed us entirely.

I gathered dry branches and was ecstatic that I brought matches with me. Rummaging through my backpack, I found a bottle of wine that I had completely forgotten about.

"We're saved!" I declared when the fire had begun to blaze, and I had managed to push the cork into the bottle. We raked together a small hillock of dry grass and sat on it in front of the campfire.

"I just didn't bring any glasses," I said.

"Now I'll be able to find out your thoughts," she laughed. "If people drink out of the same container, they can read each other's thoughts."

It was good that it was dark and that the reflections of the campfire didn't give a complete impression of the color of my face at that instant.

Liza gulped and her lips turned black – this was the local blackberry wine that I hadn't seen for sale in the *Silpo* store or in the stores in town.

"That's really tasty! The real thing," she said. "I've never had any like that before!"

I was ready to wag my tail and stand on my back paws.

"You know I've always wanted to taste that kind of wine," Liza continued, staring into the fire, "but it seemed to me that these kinds of wine – in faceted black bottles – are kept just in the cabins of drowned pirate ships… A kind of miracle!" She had another gulp and stretched out the bottle to me. "Good, guess what I'm thinking!"

I drank it up and began to "guess":

"You came here because… you can't go to Spain!"

"Precisely – to Spain!" She cheerfully confirmed and again exclaimed. "A charming wine! Go on further!"

I took another swig:

"You're itching to eat a great big bloody cutlet, fried on a charcoal grill!"

"With pepper and rock salt!"

I slurped some more:

"You're a witch! You're right at home!"

She burst into laughter and the forest responded with a similar sound. She took the bottle from me:

"That's enough. Now my turn!"

A gulp:

"You've fallen in love with me."

A gulp:

"You're fearful…."

A gulp:

"You're all aquiver because…."

I took the bottle from her and unexpectedly threw it into the bushes. Liza once again burst out laughing. Damned wine! Where did I get it? From some village lady near the store…."

"That's enough," said Liza, "let's try to sleep before the fire goes out."

She got her sweater out of her bag, stretched it out and, huddling up, lay down on a pile of hay. I took my coat, covered her legs and settled next to her in such a way that, God forbid, I might touch her. But could I fall asleep? I observed her through my squinting eyes and after a certain amount of time with astonishment noticed that she had actually fallen asleep. As though she were sleeping in her warm bed at home. The flames in the campfire were munching the remains of the branches that were smoldering in it and finally died out. I drowned in the darkness and began to listen carefully to sounds: to hear if a bear or wolf would suddenly come upon us... I needed to be on guard! And also... it was awfully vexing for me to be lying next to this strange girl, who had so quickly and easily fallen asleep. She didn't take me seriously at all. Maybe I acted like a fool all day. Though I was also thinking about something else: all the same I wouldn't dare touch her! At least not now....

5.

In the morning we were already lying really close to one another. This happened accidentally. The cold woke me up, and I saw that her hands, touchingly clenched into little fists, pressed to my chest. I grew still, made it look like I was sleeping. And later I actually fell asleep one more time (the reason for which I couldn't forgive myself later!). I woke up from a movement next to me. Liza was sitting with her back to me and was combing out her hair, then she slowly began to braid it. My heart started: it seemed as if we had been living in this forest for an eternity! We had been together for a long time, and I had always been following this morning ritual of weaving braids. There just remained for me to snuggle up to this girl with a natural and familiar movement... Why isn't life a movie that you can edit at your discretion?! It will be that way, say, after a year I surmised, then why lose valuable time? What would my old friend Myshko do in my place? He would have just grabbed her there by the shoulders, pulled her toward himself, and would have said something like:

"Are you frozen, my little morsel? Horrible! And... he'd get a slap in the face. Or he might not get one if it were not she, not Elizaveta Tenetska. There remained for me only to observe her agile fingers sliding through the strands. Then she turned around.

"You're up? Are you frozen?"

"A little. And you?"

"Well, you warmed me up so well all night!" She laughed. "Run get the bottle. We'll warm up. Don't worry, in the morning wine loses its magic!"

I had to crawl into the bushes and search out the magical libation. Liza pulled out some baked goods out of her bag, and we "filled the hole a little." When we had completely gathered our things, we tidied ourselves up, and for the last time looked at our little nocturnal refuge.

"I'll never forget this," I said.

"You will...," Liza disagreed and added, "Though in general it was nice, but now we have to somehow get out of here. And as fast as possible. I'm sure they're looking for us.

But it didn't turn out to be "as fast as possible." We walked for half a day more. This time she really got tired, and I took her by the hand. Again we went down and up the steep slopes. The forest and mountains encircled us like a carousel.

At about five o'clock the sky was covered in dark storm clouds, the air became wet, like a rag that you need to squeeze out, the earth beneath our feet became muddy.

"A downpour's going to start now," Liza said. "We need to get into the valley."

We quickened our pace. The descent was steep, but through the thick shrubbery we saw some kind of farmstead and quickly moved toward it. In the yard the owner in canvas pants rolled up to his knees was fussing about – an old guy who liked to avoid people. He was quickly raking up hay and covering the stacks with tarps. Our presence there, of course, didn't bother him at all. The black sky had already come close to the earth itself and from there, lightning streaks fell out in armfuls of golden vipers.

"Will you let us in to wait out the storm?" I asked.

"This storm is an all-nighter," the old guy angrily replied, "and I just have one bed in the house...."

"Then let us into the loft," I nodded in the direction of the wooden building that reminded me of a cattle shed or chicken coop.

"There are chickens below...."

"And upstairs?" Liza asked with hope.

"Hay is upstairs... I'm afraid you might set fire to it."

The sky had already sagged and hung low like a plastic bag filled with water. The tiniest hole was enough for a waterfall to gush out on us. Liza was shivering. She, for sure, had caught a chill. I pulled out of my pockets all the money I had, took the watch off my hand and a gold chain – a gift from my mother – from my neck. I shoved all this into the hands of the owner of the place. He distrustfully cast a glance at me, considering the treasure in his palms. Then I also took off my jacket – it was completely new. The old guy shoved it under his arm, waved his hand in the direction of the cattle shed and, tossing his rake, ran into the house.

"If you want milk or bread – come over in the morning!" He shouted to us already from the window.

Just as we crossed the threshold of our hiding place, a worldwide flood began to peal behind our backs. The chickens were already sleeping and discontentedly were clucking in their sleep, pressing to one another. They looked like white ghosts. I helped Liza get up into the loft. It was stuffed almost to the ceiling with fragrant hay. We sank into it as though into a cloud. We heard heavy as stones droplets of rain stamping along the roof. Liza lay down on her back. Her breathing was heavy. I carefully touched her palm. It was cold. She didn't draw back her hand from me… I grew emboldened and raised her hand to my lips. A wave of tenderness covered me – a strange, unfamiliar to me tenderness that was mixed with despair.

"You won't disappear?" I asked.

She turned on her side, and for a moment we looked at each other. Her eyes floated before me like two wet tiny blue fish. I pressed her to me. But she pushed herself away:

"Listen, I don't want to mess with your head. Hardly can you consider this all chance. I understand a bit of this…."

"Of course it's not chance. This can't be chance…," I sighed, kissing her arm higher and higher, "I've been dreaming about you from the first day I met you!"

"Wait a minute!" She sharply straightened herself up and sat down opposite me with her legs crossed. "I don't need all this. Do you understand?! And you don't need this. How old are you – eighteen? I'm almost ten years older than you."

"What does that mean?" I couldn't understand.

"For this night, of course, nothing," she agreed, "but for you, I'm sure, that won't be enough. Do I understand correctly?"

"Yes. Most likely, I'm a one-woman man."

"There, you see. Why should I ruin your life? All of it's ahead of you…"

"With you!"

"No. First, I have a child…."

"That's wonderful!"

"Second, my life, to which I've gotten used to, I'm not about to change in any way. This moment will pass, and then you'll begin to pursue me, demand something… And I've gotten weary of all that. I don't need it. Do you understand?"

But I didn't understand anything.

Then in fragmentary flashes, like that first evening, I saw just her light, translucent outline that hovered above me. Everything got entangled. The rain and wind rocked the barn like a boat, the hay rustled and I embraced her together with armfuls of the dry, fragrant grass. She was the very grass that intoxicated me, that scratched me from head to toe till I bled, that came on my back and elbows....

I told her that I'm a one-woman man. But then I still didn't know that it was the truth.

ELYZAVETA TENETSKA

1.

She returned to the city earlier than she had planned. Tired, chilled and irritated. But if you can't bear the whole collective thing, then elbow your way on that hike? Her bones still ached from the trip in the cart, in which the landlord of the barn drove her and the student to the tourist resort. As it turned out, they had walked quite far, since the cart had rumbled its way through the forest and mountains for about two hours. At the tourist resort they hushed up the adventure. The strange little pair turned out to be overly silent: the student was in a state of incomprehensible euphoria, the lady waved off the nurse, who had approached her with a thermometer... And what a look she had at that moment! Why would she need this kind of rest at all? She had yielded to the persuasion of her girlfriend, and here you see the result: the very same tedium. Just a romantic incident was added to it. No, you have to resolve something with yourself.

From September on she was supposed to work in the department, teaching something, putting herself out before the green first-year students, knowing that every one of her words will be soaked in falsehood. And the boys and girls under the conditions that exist today, would never film their version of *Andrei Rublev*. But then – forget about it? And also the thought disturbed her that in all likelihood, *that* one could be among the students. It was difficult to imagine a more brutal situation! Liza ascended the third floor, pulled the key to her apartment door out of her pocket. It was dark and quiet in the long corridor, the neighbors hadn't come home yet from work. Liza pushed the door of her apartment – she didn't lock it, threw her suitcase on the threshold and walked up to the bed. She sat down. It smelled of dust in the room, as always happens when owners are gone for a long time. She needed to phone her mother and ask her to bring her daughter Lika[9] home toward evening, so she'd have a chance to tidy up, run to the store for bread and milk, and make her something tasty to eat….

Summer was over… It was short and flashed past almost unnoticeably. Liza recalled what hopes she has placed on it. Over the course of the year negotiations continued about including her in a delegation travelling to a conference in Madrid. She needed to collect an incredible pile of documents, including medical ones, to make the rounds of hundreds of abominable offices, where each clerk tossed a skeptical look at her, and routinely asked her: "Do you possibly intend to remain abroad?"

Some suggested discussing this question "over a shot" somewhere in a quiet foreign currency bar – a special place that was accessible just for the chosen few. And finally, when everything seemed to have worked out, the department head called her in and, his eyes wandering along the wallpaper of his own office, explained that there, "up there," suddenly they found out that she had a child from a "person of doubtful loyalty," who was serving a term for anti-government statements. "My child," he said, "You needed to inform us about this right away. Because it looked like you intentionally hid this fact. Now it's too late to change anything. If there just hadn't been a child… You didn't register your marriage, did you?"

---

9   Pronounced "Leeka."

That was true. When at home they found out that Liza was communicating with dangerous individuals and she had already been called in for conversations "with the proper authorities," her mother said: "You got what you asked for!" And when it became clear that she was also pregnant, she added harshly: "You've run around...." It made little sense to explain anything. It would have required far too many words and effort, and she preferred a preponderance of silence.

After the exit exams at the institute, her favorite teachers, noticing her overly round belly, told her when they were alone:

"It's going to be hard for you. And not even over the child. The fact that you've decided to keep it – good. Remember – you're really talented. And you have to stand out – be more patient, endure more. For the time being stay in graduate school, and then we'll see. Time changes things. Take care of your child, put your life in order – that's also very important. And – wait. Maybe, in just a short time...."

Little Lika was now two years old. Not that much time had already passed. And patience had come to an end. This particularly became understandable after her Madrid trip was turned down. Not to speak about the destruction of her film *Madness* and several other movies that only her fellow classmates had seen. First and foremost she took care of Lika.

She always knew she'd have a little girl with that name! Once long ago in her childhood, Liza and her grandmother were on vacation in a pension on the shore of the Sea of Azov. It seemed she was eleven at the time, with not a single girl her age around her. Back then she befriended a fourteen-year-old girl on the beach. More precisely, the girl approached her. At first Liza discontentedly fanned away her persistent questions, then later – took interest. And after some time a marvelous thing happed: the tiny girl turned out to be a clever girl and a big daydreamer. The girl's name was Lika.

"Anzhelika?" Liza kept asking her, "Angelina? Likera?"

"No, Lika!" The little girl insisted.

It was hard to remember about what they were talking back then, but Liza was left with the strange impression that she had met a tiny angel, who knew how to speak simply about complex things. For fun, Liza posed to the child the most complex questions that she herself was thinking about: "Is there a God?," "How did the first person appear on Earth?", and even about the structure of the universe – and the little girl delivered such masterpieces of answers, that it would have been valuable to jot them down. She didn't. And now she had forgotten completely. Just the name remained – Lika.

Lika is a little girl, a child of such a short-lived and burning love, she's the reliable anchor that's keeping her by the shore. She was born to a Mozart melody that flowed out of the hospital's speaker – just as easily as that music did a hundred years ago. And it seemed to Liza that she was wearing not an unwashed hospital shirt with a giant slit on her stomach, but Venetian lace. These few days that she spent in the maternity ward were the happiest days of her life. Nothing got in the way of this feeling – not the cockroaches shuffling along the walls, not a burst blood vessel in her eye, not the chitchat of her three roommates in the room, who were endlessly complaining about their husbands. She wanted her daughter to be like the Lika from her childhood. When the nurse carried out the infants – one in each arm – Liza immediately recognized hers: from beneath the standard bonnet, she could see chestnut-colored locks.

"It turned out to be a lovely little girl!" The nurse said, "and so calm… She'll probably be a professor…."

Now her entire life was devoted to Lika and… waiting. And in it there was no room for anyone else! And even more so – for some student.

In most recent times she noticed that nothing external interested her. She, like a sponge, soaked up into herself all the juices of the surrounding world and that world – in a better, modified form – perfect and just, existed inside her. Everything that happened externally, including not many romances, Liza accepted like a droplet of iodine in a glass of clear water. The world that she built inside her ("You have to endure! Times will change…") wasn't in the air. It was waiting for its time…."

2.

…Problems began with the first day of classes. She entered the classroom and immediately stumbled upon eyes. His eyes. The student was sitting in the first row and didn't take his attentive gaze from her. It was unbearable. Even more so, because she had to appear in front of the students in her new capacity as the course supervisor. At first it seemed to her that those eyes were staring at her quite brazenly and ambiguously. But with each minute that impression disappeared. Like a person who got used to understanding the tiniest shades of feelings, Liza sensed that in those eyes there was no aggression, arrogance or the least vulgar hint about the August adventure. It was as if the gaze of the student enveloped her in a protective aura, guarded her. And she calmed down. At the end of the class, during which she gave the first-year students the syllabus, explained a certain amount of the routine, and stated her introductory comments, he stepped up to her among several others – mostly girls – and, waiting until her fervent lament gushed out and they scattered, said to her:

"I'd like to invite You… er you… over to my place. Is that possible?"

She sternly knit her brows:

"No. I hope that's clear? Or are there going to be any problems?"

He nearly was covered in frost, as though from the breath of a glacial ocean; beads of perspiration even appeared on his forehead.

"And I request that You," Liza added, "use my name and patronymic like everyone. Otherwise… Otherwise I'll be forced to quit my job tomorrow. Agreed?"

He nodded.

"Good. I'll be waiting. As long as I have to…."

"Unnecessary trouble!" She shut her planning book and quickly moved in the direction of the door, and looked back at him in the doorway. "Don't get stupid thoughts in your head, young boy! All your life's before you."

In general that was it. Liza stayed in the department office until two o'clock and got ready to go home.

She walked through the city as though she were in a fog, heavily tearing through a cloud of cotton wool that drew up on her in large, thick rags. She could have dropped in at the Movie Building, drink some coffee, meet her friends, stay in their company till seven o'clock (at seven her mother brought Lika home), but then her head would be heaped up with countless unnecessary trifles and problems, her evening would be spoiled. But what was she to do till seven? Liza felt as though she were a lonely rowboat that senselessly was knocking against a foreign shore. A thirst for life stirred in her like… like kidney stones. If she could just dissolve them, break them up inside her. Then her entire essence would become filled with happy little balloons and she would fly off together with them there, where… "Where – just where?" She thought. There where joy reigns, the natural joy from being, from delight in the wind, wine, the scent of the forest… "It will be that way!" Liza said to herself. But just not right now, not now. The mysterious forest – fresh and mirthful, with clear streams and abundant wild cherries will still accept her into its embraces. She just needed to wait. Suddenly she began to suffocate from a recollection of the scent of the hay there, in the loft, in the cattle shed-chicken coop… The little boy student promised to wait. To wait for what? What's the difference? It was she who was waiting. So let him wait. Liza decided to go to the coffee shop – her favorite one that was located on the second floor of the town's bathhouse. Instead of instant coffee, they made real coffee there – Turkish style, on hot sand in ceramic Turkish pots, and there were always few people there. Only those who knew about the existence of this unusual little spot for sauna lovers.

Liza carefully took her espresso coffee cup and held it in her palm: they broke off the handles on purpose here (so people wouldn't steal them!) and sat down at a little table that was in the furthest corner of the room. The coffee shop was almost empty. The time was kind of in-between: for those who like to sit and chat for the evening get-together – too early, for the usual morning ritual – too late. With satisfaction Liza took a gulp and involuntarily looked at the doorway entrance – several years ago her "dubious" company used to gather here. Now she didn't know who was where… Stop! Liza strained her eyes, looking over the silhouette of a woman in the darkness, who had just entered.

She wasn't mistaken. This really was the heroine of her film that had been destroyed, a talented actress, who, after many triumphs fell out of sight. Liza had heard of rumors of her stormy romance with a well-known director, about his tragic death, of which they accused her; they even kept her for three years in a hard labor penal colony, and she also had started to drink heavily.

Three years of being so conspicuous made a mark on her external appearance, her gait, the way she carried herself, but the gesture, which the woman used to fix her hair, remained the same – elegant, as though in her life there never had existed the dark blue barracks uniform or the boots made of tarpaulin.

The actress (Liza respectfully called her Anastasiya Yuriyevna) surveyed the room and unmistakably moved directly at her table. Liza stood up and moved toward her, they silently hugged each other, stood there for a minute to the surprise of the other customers, until the painful moment of their meeting turned into an awkward moment. They sat down at the table.

"You haven't changed at all, my dear," the actress said, "twenty-five years, twenty-eight years – I don't see a difference. At that age a woman can look the same, even look younger… But at my age… But – for God's sake! – without compliments! Everyone's giving me compliments today, as though I've walked out of a beauty salon instead of prison.…

As always, she spoke a lot and didn't listen much to her interlocutor. This struck Liza even at the movie shoots: others were tense, repeated their lines, warmed up to their roles, or intently remained silent, and she acted like she were spilling out of herself everything in excess, like water from a tin can with thick oil. Liza knew her from childhood from her movies and theatrical roles – she mostly played princesses in children's fairy tales, delicate "Turgenevian" girls and "Arbuzov"[10] maximalists. Her sweet flat nose, her tidy round face, her tiny little arrow brows and – grace in every movement. When Liza entered the theatrical institute, posters with portraits of this star were plastered all over the city. While she was at school, Liza made some extra money as a costume maker. Sometimes on days off when the actresses weren't there, she would dress in their dresses and would prance in front of the mirror. One time at that moment she entered, the prima donna. It's true that then she already was no longer a delicate angel and, as people gossiped, quietly took to drinking after the death of her three-year-old son, remaining at the same time a particularly tragic romantic figure, the object of gossip and courting. She had entered without making a sound and stopped directly in front of Liza:

"What gold is wasted as she languishes as a costume maker! Good heavens…," she uttered, shamelessly swallowing Liza with her great big eyes, "you're exactly

____

10 Soviet playwright Alexander Arbuzov (1908-1986).

the way I always dreamed of being – 'one who turns everything into charcoal!'"

"And You – are just the way I dreamed of being!" Liza grew emboldened to make an appropriate compliment.

"Do you know me?"

"I've seen you in the movies and on stage," Liza suddenly became interested and embarrassed at the same time: the woman who was standing in front of her was extraordinarily beautiful, inaccessible. She had heard that some people called her a "genius wretch"....

Then there was *Madness*. Liza knew beforehand that Anastasiya was going to play in it. That role became the best work she would do in the movies. The best and… last.

"Do you drink or are you a righteous woman?" The actress interrupted her recollections. "Maybe you'll buy me a drink?"

Liza walked up to the barkeep and bought a glass of cognac. The actress's face became flushed. She drained it in a single gulp. Liza became sad.

"Are you making anything right now?" Anastasiya asked her.

"Nothing. I stayed in the department. I'm working."

"Ah, you're a smart girl," her interlocutor for some reason became glad. "Maybe you'll survive… For those like you it's better to sit quietly, like a mouse…," the actress in an unsure movement raised her finger to her lips and Liza with horror understood, that she just needed a thimbleful to get drunk. "They'll eat you alive, they'll eat you up. If not those who are jealous, then men will. But, you know what I'm saying to you – don't let yourself be broken. You can bend, but this way, so it's not in half and not with a crack – no! It's not the time for those like us, not the… Here I was born 'Nastasiya Pylypypivna,'[11] and what do I see: a trifle, quarrels, sweaty palms… Make a Dostoevsky film

---

11   The tragic heroine from Dostoevsky's novel *The Idiot* Nastasya Filippovna.

sometime, eh? Not right now, but sometime later… I'll at least play a kitchen table for you! Promise?"

"Of course, Anastasiya Yuriyevna. It just won't be soon…."

"When it happens – then give me a call…," her voice suddenly took on an aggressiveness, "and if it doesn't happen – then it serves you right! It means you were born to be a costume maker and – you'll die a costume maker! Let's have another drink if you don't mind the money… Liza once again ordered a cognac.

"And now – go!" The actress said, stooping over the glass.

"Forgive me…."

"For what?" Anastasiya cast a glance at her, "I've, possibly, played in earnest only in your movie. For that I'm not sorry to croak. But I won't croak. That's it, go, go… I become bad when I drink too much…."

Liza rose up. In the doorway she again glanced back in the dimly lit café. The actress continued to sit there, drooping her head low and crossing her still shapely legs in coarse stockings under the table. There was an arrow-like run on one of them. That arrow seemingly cut Liza's heart in two.

3.

…Mother brought Lika home a little earlier. The little girl sat on a little rug and was drawing something on paper, uttering something like "plya-plya." Liza knew that in translation this meant "to write." Liza quietly stopped at the doorway. She looked at the round fluffy little head with soft, nearly birdlike, hair. It stuck out in every direction, opening up a thin little neck with a dark little cavity in the middle. The little girl's head was stooped over and this underscored her puffy little cheek, from behind of which you nearly couldn't see her little snub nose. But her long, like a doll's, eyelashes were gorgeous. The little girl intently passed the pencil over the paper and rarely sighed from her effort. Liza called out to her. The little girl instantly looked back, and her face shone with a carefree smile. Liza couldn't decide – was she pretty? The features of her face were overly small – a tiny nose, a neat, distinctly traced little mouth, greenish-azure eyes. Her high brow encircled by reddish curls made her face disproportional.

They looked over each other for a minute. Finally Lika knit her brow and explained: "Plya-plya!" She was "writing." With understanding Liza nodded and closed the door....

DENYS

1.

I couldn't wait for the beginning of classes. Suddenly everything seemed petty and secondary – entering the institute, and dreams about fame....

She left so unexpectedly, earlier than anticipated by the term of her travel pass, she virtually escaped. When I found out about this, an emptiness fell on me. The kind of sensation as though an important organ had been cut out. I looked like a butterfly with a broken wing: I flapped, trying to fly up, and was able only to comically and vainly whip up dust beneath me. Would it always be like this, I thought in despair. The forest no longer enticed me. I became uninteresting for my friends and tried to stay as far away from them as possible. I barely waited out the end of the term there and took the first morning bus to the regional center in order to get on a train sooner.

I hoped that she would call (I left her my phone number because she didn't give me hers), and the last week before the beginning of classes stupidly stayed at home. At night I would look at the moon – so round and flat, like the surface of a mirror. I watched it rise up above the tops of trees and roofs, intersecting the sky and slowly dissolving in the gray skirt of the morning. How many of these moons would have to promenade along the horizon until my expectations would be fulfilled? There was no answer. I was fearful of looking for her at the institute.

…When she entered the room and quickly and indifferently glanced at me, I understood that nothing would happen. But when she said that I "shouldn't get stupid thoughts in my head," I decided to wait. To wait as long as I needed to. I knew that this wouldn't be easy. But intuitively I sensed: I can't rush. At first I even liked cultivating the sorrows of "a young Werther" inside myself. In the end, I was romantic, I got interested in the poetry of Alexander Blok and had nothing against the appearance of a Beautiful Lady in my life. And not the mythical image, but one like this – real and accessible. For several weeks provocative memories about her accessibility were enough for me. All I did was review in my memory every minute of that night and caught myself on the thought that I was doing this like… a movie maker, and not like a lover. It was important for me to regenerate that "tape," and not feelings. When I recreate it with accuracy to the second and confidently fix it in my imagination, I thought, then I'll give in to sensory perception. Maybe, then, he awakened in me, who, according the words of Blok, "takes away the scent from a flower"… I even grew angry at myself when, regenerating the next excerpt from my recollections (here a lightning streak intersects the sky and in its flash the bronze bend of a thigh appears…), I was covered in sweat and was losing my reason. I had to go over everything in my head anew.

I woke up empty and broken, lazily had breakfast and wandered to the institute without any enthusiasm.

"You were dreaming so much about your studies! What else can you ask for?" My mother one time couldn't take it. "Remember, how much effort that admission to the university cost you! Moreover, if you get good grades, your father will have more grounds to make arrangements about freeing you from army service."

On hearing the last words, his father with dissatisfaction knit his brow, and his mother flung herself at him:

"Yes, yes! And you don't have to puff and blow – we have just one son! Remember what happened with Vira's boy… Denys will go to the army just over my dead body!"

They began to argue and I evaporated from the apartment….

2.

I didn't restore the film with memories… Sounds, scents, sweet moments of giddiness got in the way, in which I generally grasped nothing. And, accordingly, I couldn't paint anything in my imagination. I abandoned this mistaken and exhausting pursuit. I returned to reality, in which she was sitting at a table in the dining hall, left the institute, walked through the city, stopped by in stores or coffee shops. I began to follow her. I walked at a good distance behind her so that – God forbid – she might notice me. I learned her daily schedule of classes, I saw how every Saturday she went for a walk with her daughter – a cute red-headed little frog, I knew that her favorite coffee shop was in the building of the town's public bathhouse. One time, when she had left there, I, abandoning my tailing of her, went inside and tried to guess at which table she was sitting. I guessed unerringly – by the brand of her cigarette butt that I… put into my pocket.

The next stage of my madness was cynicism. That is, I tried to produce it inside me the way a snake makes poison. This was my personal method of psychological training. I surmise Freud himself would have welcomed me. Again I turned over fragments of my August adventure in my memory, but this time in an entirely different perspective. This was rather difficult. What actually happened, I pondered. An ordinary summer fling, no – a tiny love affair, worse – a banal little intrigue, even more accurately – a one-time thing, sex… The whim of a woman who was bored, a single losing party in ping-pong. When it came to the various slippery little words that one would use to call what happened between us on the mountain, I gnawed my pillow with my teeth. To destroy everything definitively, I needed to make the next step: to tell two or three of my classmates about the adventure. Additionally, be drunk as a skunk and pepper my words with foul language, paint her body in intimate details and the way she trembled in my arms and begged me to meet her secretly in her apartment... Maybe this acid rain would destroy my illness forever. But I couldn't do it – I'd have to destroy myself.

How I could rid myself of the troublesome idea and reach a state of equilibrium, I didn't know. I met with my previous girlfriends several times. But this led to a new shock: I didn't feel anything! That is, in a physical sense everything was okay, I didn't lose my technique. But with horror I discovered in myself a new type of impotence: everything happened automatically. I was a robot, who was making hormones – nothing more. After those rendezvous I strove to at least feel tenderness for my partner, remembering her arms, legs, thighs and pink knees, but the feeling wasn't there. But instead of that, something completely extraneous fell into my thoughts: I remembered the stain on the wallpaper, the buzzing of a fly, the image on the kilim....

I remembered the wine, that damned old lady's wine that Liza called "enchanted."

I hated everything linked with superstitions, but right at that moment I was frightened like a girl: and what if the old lady who had sold that wine on the sly was really a witch? And her wine – some kind of "magic potion" with which she's trying to reduce all men to naught?

...After a month, when all the others were assiduously making summaries of all the boring lectures of the instructors, which seemed to me to be complete idiocy, I sensed a certain relief: hate and the thirst for any kind of activity. I sauntered through the streets and pondered what I should do. Thrash the store windows? Write political slogans on the walls, something like "Freedom for this or that one"? Shout out poems on the crossroads or be met with a knife in a dark entryway? I precisely remember that I wanted hospital orderlies to wrestle me down so that pink spume would come out of my mouth with insensible words, so that they'd prick me with needles of tranquilizers and lock me up in a ward where I could freely smack my head against the wall... I didn't need any other life. I lost sense of it. The fame that I was dreaming about turned into a handful of mud that had flown into my face. Why and for what reason did I need her, I pondered, thinking about this not for the first time. I remembered the folktale "Ruslan and Ludmilla" – a touching childhood nostalgia with the voice of my mother who bent over me, sick with tonsillitis, and fervently recited Pushkin's lines. On the other hand it was strange that I remembered a secondary hero, who was accomplishing a bunch of heroic acts and, already turned into an old sorcerer, heard from Naina one and the same thing: "I don't love you!" I wasn't a little old man, I was young, filled with strength and plans, but those four words completely knocked me out of life.

...In the spring they started to take guys my age into the army. A lot of my classmates had already served (they were given preference for acceptance into our department), so it was my turn. I observed my parents fall silent, they locked themselves in the kitchen and spoke in low tones for a long time, my mother was sobbing, my father was coming home late and not very sober, and my mother didn't even argue with him. It was even just the opposite – she was getting from her girl friend (the same one whose son died last year) imported liquor and in the morning putting them in my father's suitcase. And again he's going somewhere "into battle." However, I wasn't upset by this until they solemnly notified me that I was freed from army service! It was just then that my madness receded....

The army! That's my way out. I need to go, get up at the sound of a bell (or trumpets, the devil knows how they do it, run on the striped square, fall face first into mud, get up and fall again, to do pushups from the floor, to give in to someone's will, in the same way witnessing my transformation into a robot, a mechanism, into an object for officially permitted cruelties.

In the morning I rushed to the military registration office. And in the evening I endured a weighty conversation with my parents that ended with the calling for an ambulance for my mother....

I courageously endured the stupid ritual under the name of "seeing-off," without sitting any of my female admirers next to me. I listened to the solemn instructions of my father, neighbors, classmates, I had a lot to drink, and I exchanged kisses with who knows... I wanted to get rid of all this as soon as possible. Then I rode in a train car, looked at the shorn backs of the heads of yesterday's school boys, my new friends, and I smirked. I was riding away from her. I was nearly happy – a deaf and blind piece of biomass, divested of feelings, who thirsted for one thing – to be killed. Or… to kill.

When after quick training near Bishkek, they announced to us they were sending our unit to Afghanistan – a calm finally descended on me. It was exactly what I needed…

Irene Rozdobudko

PART TWO
DENYS
December 1994

1.

A week before the New Year I received an invitation to work in the capital. Negotiations about the transfer of a "talented film script writer and video clip maker" were conducted with a producer's television agency for a long time. But at first I wasn't enamored of the fact that I had to live with my parents. Only when my employers informed me that they had agreed to buy me an apartment not far from downtown did I agree. And now I was seeing the old year out in my one-room apartment, where I've been living after my assignment to this already not that small, but, all the same, provincial city.

I needed to gather my thoughts and generally – get my act together, that's why I cut off all relations with the external world. I just went to work, signed some papers and hid from calls from my temporary acquaintances. I didn't have any friends. In this city there remained a woman, whom I didn't dare marry, and I felt unbearable guilt over this. Over these years everything got mixed up in my head, turned into a kasha, and now I needed to understand everything, to raise the line beneath these nearly idly lived years....

Beyond the window slowly long spirals of snowstorms rolled out and hung to the ground, they were similar to bandages. It seemed that there, above, lies a wounded giant. I had just turned thirty-five... A good – if not the biggest – chunk of my life remained behind me. What was in it? One could say with certitude that I'm a "lucky man." Usually people hate these kind, they are attracted to them just to draw energy from them and go further....

…In Afghanistan they didn't off me, and I requested a second tour of duty, and when I successfully served it, remained for a third. They looked at me like an idiot or – total garbage. True, I didn't feel very normal. It was as if in my head a giant reel with a movie tape was turning, onto which I recorded actions with detachment. The only thing that didn't grab me was lying in a foreign town square with an open groin like Seryoga from Shepetivka. More precisely, I'm fine with "in the middle of the town square," but that open groin… A skull carried off like Mykolka's from Lugansk also didn't grab me. In general, death itself wasn't the most awful, but rather the thought about what they'll do with you after – they'll drag you in a tarp to an earthen hut that's called "the morgue." They'll sprinkle you with disinfectant or with some kind of disinfecting solution… But this is in the best case scenario, when your body is picked up by your own guys. Understanding that you've ended up in global disarray, almost in the Middle Ages, I, as earlier, mostly turned my attention to details, thinking that they at least have some kind of sense. That is why my memory fixed many different things that still torment me at night: a rat cut in half (he ran along the edge of an improvised table right at that moment when we were downing pure alcohol, in memory of Serhiy, and our senior lieutenant struck it with a cutlass, as though the death of our comrade had become embodied in that creature), a rose-colored nipple that shone in the slit of a formless pile of rags that covered what once was a human being, the lustfully-frightened eyes of Zulfika (the half-crazed Pashtun tribeswoman who for some reason was accompanying us) at that moment, when Tymokhin was making his "fourth approach" to her… Three of my short-term leaves I spent not far from Bishkek. I wasn't thirsting to see clean bedding and the scenery of the banks of the Dnipro River from the windows of my bedroom. I didn't see myself in this life.

My parents overwhelmed me with letters. And only then, when they unexpectedly grew silent, I decided that it was time to return. I rejected an assignment to the military academy, which really surprised the commanders, and I set off for home.

On the road I read Hemingway, smoked some grass in the bathrooms of trains and thought that I was a typical representative of the "lost generation...."

2.

I returned in the spring, and in the summer, at the request of my parents, signed up again to the Institute. This didn't require any great efforts as it did six years ago – I just put on my uniform. "Green freshmen" surrounded me, among which I recognized my previous self... Of course I tried to find out about Elyzaveta Tenetska. On the first day of classes, walking along the corridor, I mused about meeting her. Though just a day before I was sure that I had cut off this slice of my life forever. Nothing of the sort! I mused about meeting her anyway. Ravings! And all the same I knew now that everything might be different. I was no longer a spoiled little boy, I looked considerably stronger. I was sure that I'd be able to take her by the hand even if she doesn't want me to. But my expectations turned out to be in vain – in the department they said that Tenetska hasn't been working there for a while. And where she was – no one knew. She didn't live at her old address, and I didn't have the new one... The café was no longer there in the public washroom building on the town square. The bathhouse also was no longer there. Some kind of bank branch had taken over the building.

I was filled with hate then. With a sense of disgust I saw that life hadn't changed and even had become livelier, that that little island of blood and filth, which I inhabited – for the local inhabitants was nothing more than "myths and legends of the peoples of the world." Additionally I felt with my skin an unhealthy interest of people in me. "Did you have to kill anyone?" My classmates asked me and greedily awaited my answer. One time the thought came to me that she, Liza, would ask me the same thing. A single word. "Hero, I don't love you!"…

I studied the requisite five years. I won't say that I forgot her and didn't look for her. I looked. Till the time when I came to the conclusion: in the end, everyone aspires for just one thing – love, saying it in a different way – recognition. This searching can lead you just about anywhere – to terrorism, feminism, fascism, just anywhere. Whoever doesn't want to disappear into oblivion, but who doesn't have any talent, strives in any way to make himself be known. If Hitler had been recognized as a real artist, if Josef Dzhugashvilli[12] hadn't been thrown out of the seminary, would they have wanted to prove to the world that they exist in such a horrific way? What was lacking for those dirty swine, who sent the innocent Mykolka from Lugansk to his death? Maybe love? At least to their homeland….

Unlove turns a person into a leper with a bell on his neck: you can hear him everywhere, and his bell – is the sign to disperse for the rest. However, love for such an unhappy person is needed just as a goal, to which he must go in complete solitude. He must walk long, forever, and never stop. I suppose that bell with a warning hung on me as well: "Don't get close – it will kill you!" I was just a seeker, on the road, I couldn't remain in any dwelling that I came across on my path. I already was no longer dreaming of fame. Those youthful ravings were aired out of my head. I got involved with something else – I began to study, I started to keep a bunch of notebooks and folders, where I kept interesting clippings from the one foreign paper *The Times* that was sold in kiosks. I read a bunch of books for which I didn't have enough time before....

---

12   Joseph Stalin's real Georgian name.

…And then right now, planning to abandon the small town that had accepted me, I opened up my diary and, before burning it, I decided to reread parts of it.…

"You need to get used to life on the summits of mountains – so that deeply beneath you the miserable lament about politics would ring, about the egotism of nations. Indispensible is foreseeability before you can exist in the labyrinth. And… the sevenfold experience of solitude…" and further on already mine: "Nietzsche is worthy of respect at least for the fact that just a minority agrees with his anti-humanistic and anti-Christian ideas. Knowing this, he all the same remained himself."

"Compassion carries the infection of suffering – in certain conditions compassion can lead to the loss of life energy… Even if God has his hell: it is love for people!"

Then again mine: "I'll try to write down what I thought about during the night today… Nietzsche… His philosophy can be understood by people, who have gotten used to life "on the mountain peak," alienated, in his words, from "chit-chat and egotism." And he himself, like a cobbler, rails against Kant, aspiring for superiority. Every mortal, if by nature he isn't a philosopher and isn't capable of summing up reality, seeks HIS philosopher. At first I assumed I liked Nietzsche. I really like him to a certain degree – with his idea of aristocrats of the spirit and slaves, condemnation of hypocrisy. But Nietzsche salutes Buddhism, because it is a joyful religion, directed at the care of your own body, your health. That was disgusting for me. It's not interesting for me among joyful people. Long ago I've already lived through the most important, and therefore it's so difficult for me to fake some kind of emotions, to pose among others like a clown." A quote again: *"Love is the single, last chance to survive.…"*

I: "Liza I don't remember you.…" The Bible: *"Don't swear! Let your word be either "yes" or "no." Everything more than this – is from the devil. Don't judge, so that you won't be judged. For whatever judgment you will judge – with that you will be judged.…*

...the gate is tight and the road is narrow that leads to life, and there are few who find it!"

I became sad. My notes expressively pointed to the turmoil that dominated in my head. All this should remain here. Under the bathtub I found a small copper basin. I put the diary into it and carefully burned it from four sides...."

3.

I came to the city on assignment to fill a vacancy as a director's assistant. It turned out that the position didn't exist – the staff was too small, and the local TV station didn't film anything more significant than news releases and reports on the opening of new buildings. The director took pity on me and set me up working at the movie theater.

"You know something about the movies, don't you?" He asked. "Stay there a bit. And when vacancies appear – I'll give you a whistle. You're from the capital all the same – you'll be needed!"

I had to wait for his whistle for two years. I rented an apartment not far from The Banner of October Movie Theater, and I took the position of "senior specialist." My responsibilities included picking films for the theater's four screens. Every Tuesday from eight in the morning all the specialists of the city gathered in the building of the local town council and sweated there till late in the evening, choosing new films for their establishments. After the movies were ordered, I had to put together announcements and put them on the movie theater's answering machine. From that time till this day I can easily pronounce the names of all the Indian actors... "Today and all week in our movie theater see...," I enunciated clearly, knowing that hundreds of movie fanatics every day will listen to all this nonsense that I blathered into the receiver.

The community that gathered in the movie theater was quite strange – mostly women with heavy gold earrings and with unfulfilled personal lives. They all looked alike –

white hair overly burnt from a perm, bright red lips. They demanded melodramas, sobbed over *Yeseniya*, stormily discussed *Zita and Gita*, and ecstatically took care of me.

I watched the movies, read the announcements, checked the work of the artists who painted the posters (something in the spirit of Kisa Vorobyaninov[13]), and for hours roamed around the city, trying to find its most inviting corners. But such places didn't exist in it.

I didn't get paid very much. Restaurants didn't attract me any more. Judging from all this, the next step and logical consummation of the career of a "well-known movie producer" was to get married. One time I even seriously thought about it. This was a moment of despairing hunger and the disinclination to wash my sufficiently dirty sweater myself.

Did I want to return? I was indifferent.

A senseless horror from staying here could hardly be compared to my actual life in Afghanistan. Every day, besides that day, when I was supposed to be at a weekly movie screening, I sat on the second floor of the movie theater in the café and my "Thumbelinas" (as I intentionally baptized three of my subordinates, "junior specialists" – the old lady of the movie theater granny Valya, the former art critic Veronika Platonivna, and a forty-year-old beauty Rita, who looked like a gypsy) didn't bother me. I was "a person from the capital," and in addition to that – with higher education in cinematography and even – single! In a word, a holy cow. After half a year of difficult acclimatization to the city, the first woman in my life appeared. I say "first" because I stopped on the eighth one, whom I'm unfaithfully dumping. Here I read a bunch of books – romantic trash (it was still difficult to get books then, and I got bored sitting in the library) and I made a discovery: all the authors distinctly painted the exterior of their characters – the sex, color of their eyes and other attractive parts of their body,

---

13 A humorous character from Ilya Ilf's and Evgeny Petrov's comic novel *The Twelve Chairs*, which also was made into popular movies during Soviet times.

with all of which the main hero was enrapt. And, reading about this even in Flaubert, Chekhov or Balzac, I couldn't comprehend whether I was normal. But a woman, whom I could like, had to be like water… Just when I managed to distinctly describe all the virtues of some new female acquaintance for myself, my interest in her disappeared. I understood: not what I was looking for! If after a first date I couldn't put together two words about her external appearance – this was already close. Very close to that feeling that's called fondness. And… so infinitely far from my blinding bedazzlement by Liza….

4.

…Finally, this was in 1989, a director found me (now he was called a "producer") of a television company. The television network expanded and he remembered a "junior specialist" who was barely getting by in a movie theater. He offered me the position of director of the TV program City-X Culture.

I need to make note of the fact that all the inhabitations of the city were great patriots of it. Here the concepts of "X-ian mentality," "X-ian spirituality," "X-ian way of speaking" existed; in every library various cultural and religious groups gathered from "Roerich followers" to "the children of Krishna," in the exhibition halls and the "propaganda rooms" of establishments were shown the paintings of local artists exclusively on the worker's theme of "The Oath of the Steelmaker" (it's curious what kind of oath steelmakers give before they make the steel?), "Mother" (a salute to Gorky!), "Miners Who Drink Kefir" (a worthy drink for hard workers!), "The Future Mining Engineer" (where else could an adolescent apply from the working class part of town?). We needed to broadcast from the screen for precisely thirty minutes. The young anchorwoman choked in sniffles of rapture, and I didn't have any desire to do battle with this. I presumed that it would be this way forever until they bury me here in the city of Zeppo, or it will sink beneath the earth together with its mentality and Roerich-loving grannies.

Everything began suddenly. First off, for the director of a company, as the light wind of changes arrived here. An advertisement appeared. Distressed private local businessmen wanted their local citizens to find out about their products and laid out their money. After many hours of "planning sessions," at which the director – an old, tempered in verbal battles Party man, clutched his heart and beat his hoof – we've, however, gone on a different path. And they designated me as the guy in charge of all the "anti-Soviet" actions. I began to write and film TV commercials. This, in fact, gave me the opportunity to let out of myself all the poison that had accumulated in this little town. I'll never forget my first "masterpiece!" A certain furniture factory wanted to advertise its horrible armchairs. The ad had approximately the following content. An armchair appeared on screen, next to which a local citizen appeared with a badgered look. Then next to him Zheglov played by Vysotsky[14] appeared as a montage in the frame and shouted: "He'll sit. I said!" And the local citizen fell into the armchair. After this episode the clients wanted some lyricism, so just as the old guy made himself comfortable in the wonderful easy chair, butterflies burst onto the screen, and above the head of the hero a caption appeared: "If you sit down – you won't get up! Buy armchairs and chairs from the furniture factory…" I did this as a foolish trick, like a challenge. But the director of the factory really liked my work, and he gave me a white envelope right into my hands. In time there were many of those white envelopes.

I bought a long leather coat and on one of the days organized a luxurious dinner for my former female colleague "Thumbelinas." Granny Valya wiped her moved,

---

14 The widely popular countercultural Russian bard and actor Vladimir Vysotsky (1938-1980), whose lyrics were often political in nature and social commentary on Soviet society.

reddened eyes with a handkerchief, Platonivna enjoyed the imported liqueur, and sweet Rita rubbed my leg under the table with her fragrant foot. In a word, life began to start going right, fetid capitalism slowly was gaining the upper hand, and I dove headfirst into a new game, and I began to like it. When the poor director was sent off for his deserved rest, our advertising department was already covered with nasty gold plating, and tsunamis of cynicism covered the entire film group. Over the course of the next three years they literally tore us into parts, and I got clients from neighboring oblasts. I had true success when I filmed (I thought it all up and filmed it myself!) a music video clip with the participation of the daughter of a local authority. It was shown several months on all the channels, and they started phoning me from the capital.

Again I started to function like… in war. The quiet bog of the movie theater at least gave me the opportunity to feel free….

I was no longer a representative of the "lost generation," the distance of life every day increased and I needed to train my lungs. Did the taste for life appear for me? The taste for a secure life – for sure! But the main thing I understood was that I was capable of creating this life myself, with my head. This was a pleasant sensation. Earlier I couldn't even imagine that! I imagined that before long I'll be able to rise up so high that I'll have the strength, means and necessary acquaintances to finally make something valuable. And I knew exactly what it was: I'll make a film that's going to be called *Madness*… More precisely – I'll restore it. Ravings! Everything's wrong! Why can't I tell the truth till now?

I'll find Elyzaveta Tenetska and I'll offer her the chance to make that movie. It will be a business meeting with a business proposition.

…In December 1994 I planned to move to the city of my childhood. I was returning there as a victor. They offered me a massive amount of money for that time and it was anticipated that its sum would grow in direct proportion to my capacities. I was needed. They were waiting for me. I had many plans and fresh ideas. I wasn't ready to hear just one thing: "Rich guy, I don't love you!..."

DENYS
1996

1.

...I lived in a spacious two-room apartment not far from the TV center. Twice a week I went to my parents, loading up their always half-empty refrigerator with all kinds of tasty things, that I was able to get in specialty stores, and most often – from my clients.

Here I dove into a completely different life. The time of stormy meetings that avoided me in the provinces (it was quiet there like at an oasis) was already over. The time of empty stores, provocative talk shows, "money coupons," millions of cuts days before monetary reform and... TV serials. Thanks to this last factor I had more than a thicket of blackberries amount of work; each thirty-minute series was broken off into an advertising block....

I had reasons to hate myself. I wasn't the kind of person I should have been, if life had turned out differently. Together with others, I didn't swipe bars of butter from the cart that was rolled out into the middle of an empty market hall of the supermarket, I didn't cook pea soup, and I didn't talk about the outrageous prices. From a moldy Homo Soveticus, I immediately shifted to double capitalism. Like an ingenious pupil, it was as if I had jumped several grades and much passed me by. When I scraped out the bog and blood from under my fingernails in Kandahar, the guys my age were reading Ogonyok, watching *Repentance* and arguing with their superiors. In the "district little town of X," in this quiet backwater, I practically didn't know anything about political meetings, civil disobedience and student hunger strikes… I became an average man, for whom the possibility evaporated for me to tastily gorge myself and rise up not even on foot, but by escalator. So that I completely didn't lose respect for myself, in the first two years of my residence in the capital I defended my dissertation on the topic of "Manipulative Technologies in the System of Mass Communication." And again I hit the nail on the head! This was practically a new word in the advertising business, which was developing furiously. Besides my main job, I received an invitation to give classes to students twice a week at the film scriptwriting section of the film department. The female students fell in love with me. I took the best of them to the National, treated them to sushi… With indifference, indifference!

Of my previous friends just Maksym emerged to the surface, the same one with whom I vacationed at the tourist resort after my entrance exams a hundred years ago. He found me after my dissertation became a parable on the tongues of everyone in the TV business. I invited him to have dinner at The National.

When we met next to the entrance, I didn't recognize him right away. Max had changed, had become rounder. He stamped his feet awkwardly at the doorstep next to the glass doors, and noticing me, observed: "Well, old man, you're cool! Outrageous prices here!"

I shuddered. Since the time when I worked at the movie theater I couldn't stand all the talk about prices and thoughts that I'd have to live on nothing but fried squash for thirty kopecks a kilo for a few months.

"Don't worry, my treat!" I muttered and pushed the door. The concierge (in fact once an Afghan with whom I was friendly and to whom I always gave generous tips) smiled and politely held open the door, which made Max's red face get covered in spots.

I ordered a lot of tasty things, vodka and cognac. While the soft-spoken waiters were putting all that on the table, I understood that we hardly had anything to talk about.

My head was busy with a bunch of new projects that were inaccessible to Max's understanding, and he, most likely, considered me a snob and a damn bourgeois. We drank up our first one.

"What's your dissertation about?" Max asked.

I concisely laid out the essence of it, and with every word understanding that I was wasting my time – class hate raged from the eyes of my friend.

"Hear anything about our guys?" I decided to change the topic and instantly regretted it because I heard inconsolable things: one had fallen into drunkenness, and so never filmed a single frame; another left the country; another was scraping by in a funeral services office, filming weddings and funerals. Many of them plunged into politics. It turned out that after my voluntary desire to go to the army, they considered me a true hero in the class, they talked about me and were sure that I had been killed….

"By the way," I said it as naturally as I could, "what happened to our course supervisor? I don't remember what her name was – it seems it was Elyzaveta Tenetska?..."

"She hasn't been Tenetska for a long time," Max laughed. "Haven't you heard? She…," and here Max named the well-known name of a leader of one of the parties.

"That's how it goes…," I said, to keep from being silent.

"Yes, yes. At that time, it turned out, he was in prison. And now – he's a big shot!"

And seeing my complete lack of information, Max made a long political digression for me.

"And it seems that you had some problem with his wife," Max suddenly smacked himself on the knee excitedly. "Definitely! Remember? You got lost during a hike. Have you really forgotten?"

"I remember something," I answered, "but badly… Now she's a housewife?"

"Well, you're thick!" My friend got indignant. "Today she's a pretty well-known figure. They talked a lot about her especially three or four years ago when you were milking your cows in your Khatsapetivka.[15] She traveled to Lithuania during the siege of the TV center. She also traveled to the White House and to Moscow. Her films, in fact, were super. You won't drink away talent!

"And she, what was she drinking?" I didn't understand.

"But no! That's just an expression, you're really thick! The babe waited for her starry time. And she, I'll tell you, was a babe – super duper! But no one even managed to influence her when they took you to the army, and they tossed her out of the department. The girls say that she worked wherever she could. She even used to sweep up building entryways. That's the way it was…."

I became saddened. I turned away from Max and stared into the dining room.

Mostly hotel guests were sitting here – foreigners from the diaspora, neophyte "businessmen" (then you could differentiate them from others by their garish sport coats and golden chains on their fat necks) with girls that always were on duty in the hall. The foreigners made merry, grinning their spotless porcelain teeth, the businessmen guffawed, jabbing with their chopsticks into the fish and rice roulettes, the girls laughed boisterously. I thought that I hated all this, that there remained far too little room in me for love….

"Things are good for you," Max's voice reached me. "You can go to these kind of chic eateries…."

I nodded. I tried to imagine what Elyzaveta Tentetska might be like today. Maybe she's a respectable lady, a well-known director, scriptwriter… So, sooner or later we can cross paths. But, unfortunately, I won't be able to offer her anything. Much less approach her."

…I returned home at midnight. I couldn't get to sleep for a long time. It turned out that memories hadn't left me.

---

15   A small rural town in the Donetsk Oblast in Eastern Ukraine.

I remembered everything that some lucky people simply cross out of their lives. My memory was not like a sponge that you can squeeze and gather up new impressions. I remembered everything. Each memory had its button: you press it – and you're off! Mentally I pressed the button with the inscription "August. 1977. The woods."

...Before my eyes the tiny red glow of the cigarette appeared that glimmered at night like the eye of a devil. I even sensed in my mouth the taste of cheap port wine! And – the sweet quivering from the sound of a slightly hoarse voice. Then "I saw" the swimming pool with glazed blue tiles, a tanned shoulder, a wave of hair....

Further: the scent of hay, rain... Enough! I jumped out of my bed and went to the kitchen, began to smoke in the darkness, and looking through the window, I saw my little red glow blaze up in the dark water of the glass, and I turned on the light....

Here, it turns out, is the essence of the matter! She was waiting for someone. He arrived. Times changed and she was sitting high in the saddle! And my waiting was in vain, ridiculous, hopeless – "Clever guy, I don't love you!..."

But why did my life get sidetracked that August? I quietly and peacefully flew above the forests, fields and deserts, and could land there where they were really waiting for me, but I suddenly was catapulted to an unknown place at will, into another life, and wandered off in it, sinking first in blood, then in mud, then in coupons, then in cuts. And I was a little boy from an exemplary family! For such as a rule there's no reason to regret, everything for them goes according to plan to old age....

2.

There were five of us. For my team I chose (nearly in the direct sense of this word – off the street) a talented cameraman, whom I had known from my student days, as sound editor I took a senior student (she was a stout, in great big glasses, but wonderfully pleasant and serious girl, just devoted to her work), and then two drivers. I executed the duties of scriptwriter, director, editor, and producer, and along with that – spiritual teacher. We worked like slaves on a plantation, but everyone made good money, and our videos enjoyed success and won at various competitions. I tried to help all my old friends whom I had met on my path. And they accepted me. I sensed that. However I tried to keep a distance, to get less involved socially in the company of my colleagues. Conversations exhausted me, hindered me from producing ideas. I had lunch in The National, and dinner either there or at home, which my cook and cleaning woman made for me, who came twice a week. One time, after the enthusiastic comments of my cameraman, I decided to drop in for lunch at the Kino Building. That happened on the fourth of November. The weather and my mood were disgusting: outside a thick fog hung like a solid mass, like jelly, and the same kind of viscid smog-spleen filled my lungs from inside – maybe a cold was taking its grip.

I hadn't been in the Kino Building for a long time. Maybe fifteen years, or more. Its wretched interior and menu in the restaurant immediately plunged me into an even greater ennui. The semidarkness here underscored mendicancy and desolation, and the plain wax candles on the tables bore evidence of the electricity shortage rather than of creating a romantic atmosphere. But, as strange as it was, life here was swirling. At every table there were people sitting, animatedly conversing, drinking, and in general they felt unconstrained, and my mood slowly improved. Here, it was right here, on that day – somber and languid, I caught sight of Liza.

It was like… I don't even know with what to compare that moment! It happens like this in a thriller, when practically nothing is happening in a frame – they're showing the interior of a room, the camera slowly moves along the painting that's hanging on the wall, along the patterns on the wallpaper, it goes lower, lower… And the spectator already understands that on the floor, among all this luxury a body suddenly will appear, lying in a sea of blood. But the slowing down of the frame – is unbearable, the music – horrifying… I don't know why that comparison came to mind. So, at first I noticed an earring-droplet that flashed in the earlobe of a woman who was sitting not far from my table. This intolerably sharp and momentary little ray leapt into my eyes. It was strange… She back then began for me from a red glow. That is, at first there was the flash that blinded me.

The woman sat sideways to me, she had on an elegant dark dress, shoes with high heels, her hair gathered and stretched on the back of her neck, a tall neck… How did I immediately understand that this was she? That's the question, to which I can't find an answer. Why lie that I remained calm as I had planned? Yes, I strove to be calm. But that didn't depend on me. It was for a reason that I called to mind a thriller – true horror enveloped me. From the fact that finally my dream had come true – to meet her, and even more from the fact that everything I considered past, lived through and stupidly juvenile turned out to be just as painful as though a liquid bit of iron had been pressed against my chest. Could I approach her, say "hello" to her with ease? This turned out to be impossible: my heart was pounding, my legs grew weak, and I was stuck to my chair. Two shots of vodka didn't make the situation any better.

Earlier I conjectured that she would have to change dramatically – either put on a ton of weight or waste away – and then I'd look at her derisively. But even in the semidarkness it was noticeable that this woman – was beautiful, elegant and all the same unattainable. Maybe, the features of her face had sharpened, and a small spider's web of slight wrinkles covered her face like a veil – I don't know. I saw something else. That is, just as many years ago I wasn't able to adequately apprehend her external appearance, because an invisible aura existed surrounding her that blinded me as it had done earlier.

Even more, looking her over from afar, I suddenly understood that I looked for similar features in all the women who had been with me. I collected them crumb by crumb. One had a hoarse voice – and I went after it, another – smoked, a third reminded me of Liza by her height and sharp demeanor. O, Lord, I was so banal, like a little boy, who picks a fiancée who looks like his own mother!

I tried to calm down and noticed that she wasn't alone. Her female companion was sitting opposite her, face turned to me. They were animatedly conversing. So as to shift my attention, I began to look over the other woman. She was younger, with reddish hair and bright, nearly transparent grayish-green eyes – so bright, that they reminded me of an angel from the canvas of icon painters. A mouth too big for a princess-frog, a thin nose, a sharp chin. In general, everything was not particularly proportional, but sufficiently sweet.

"The Frog Princess" was in regular blue jeans and a dark sweater. The only detail that attracted attention – was a bunch of bracelets on her wrist, they melodiously clanged from the smallest movement, like Chinese wind chimes. In Liza's aura the girl seemed to me to be just as lovely, nearly a beauty. However, that didn't concern me.

A waiter walked up to their table. Liza put a banknote into the leather cover and they got up. They walked past me. I waited for several second and also got up, walking after them. I hid near the coat check, waited a bit until they put their coats on… I walked out after them. Outside on the street Liza got into her car, waved her hand to her companion and… that's it. I was left next to the road. I watched as the black Opal turned the corner.

Then I went after "The Frog Princess." I don't know why… I didn't think about it then. "The Frog Princess." seemed to be the single thread that could lead me to the clew of my unrequited expectations.

The girl had a strange gait – it was overly quick, and this added to her charm. Her purse swayed on a long chain like a pendulum. Slowly I pulled myself into that rhythm and already no longer watched where we were going – I just walked after her, trying to hit the rhythm of her steps.

3.

…She walked.

I walked after her.

I caught up to her, but she didn't run away.

She simply didn't know of my existence yet. If she knew, she would have gotten into the first microbus and would have driven off.

And I would have never caught up to her….

But we were walking – neck and neck, and a hunter's passion already had overcome me. What did I do in similar situations ten or so years ago? I rummaged in my pockets, found the keys to my apartment and office and… and threw them at her feet. She shuddered from surprise, and looked down bewildered. I managed to bend down quicker than she could:

"Young girl, have you lost your keys?" And I extended the bunch to her.

"Thank you. Sorry." In a quick movement she grabbed the keys from my palm and they instantly disappeared in the pocket of her jacket. A quick glance of harsh green eyes… A 180-degree turn. And once again her reddish locks began to dance before my eyes. That's it! What next?

Bewildered, I stared at her back. Next to the intersection her gait grew slower, and after a few more steps she completely stopped. She opened her pocketbook, she shook it. She slapped her pockets, pulled out the keys… The girl was standing with her back to me, but I understood that she was carefully looking over the bunch of keys. Then she turned and anxiously twisted her head. She noticed me and began to draw closer uncertainly.

The most varied of emotions were reflected in her eyes. When she caught up to me, her face finally acquired a correct expression: it was laughing.

"You did that on purpose?" She asked, and stretched the keys out to me.

"Yes," I wouldn't deny it.

"And what does that mean?"

I shrugged my shoulders. "The Frog Princess" smiled, sunny little bunnies were jumping in her eyes, though it was gloomy outside. But I could have staked my life on it, that the greenish rainbow membrane of her eyes shone like a small glass in a forest spring.

"I'd like to ask you out for coffee."

"I just had lunch," she just said. "And I drank coffee…."

"What can I do?" I feigned despair.

"I don't know. What do you usually do in such situations?"

"That is?..."

"You're a great fibber. There must be some other option…."

"Of course!" I came to my senses. "There's also – tea, ice cream, the movies, the circus, bowling, pool…."

"Then I choose pool!" She exclaimed.

"Wonderful!" I took her by the hand, and with my free one flagged down a taxi that right then was passing by us.

We had barely gotten into the back seat when rain began to drum into the windshield. She laughed and squeezed my hand:

"You've just saved me!"

She was candid and direct, like a cheerful puppy.

I saw through to her core. She was whole and true, like… an apple that was filled with life's juices and with utter childhood joy. And I also thought that Liza would forever remain for me woven from molecule-signs and never would become something weightier than a droplet of water, the glimmering of a fire or the scent of leaves....

I took my new friend to the club, where besides the usual restaurant, there was a room with pool tables. I watched her play with abandon, the way she unrestrainedly jumped around the table, the way she comically stuck out the tip of her tongue when she was aiming at the ball. After a few hours I even got tired, but she was relentless until she learned to drive the ball into the pocket. Then I suggested to her that we have dinner. I knew that in this particular restaurant they prepared an incredible Irish-style steak and ordered two portions with vegetables. Everything was as if we had been old friends. That troubled me a little, but she felt completely natural, though she didn't look like a feather brain – she didn't flirt, she conducted herself with composure and in a friendly way. And when they brought the steak, she actively took part in the venture. It was pleasant for me to watch her eat – with an appetite, and with an expression of authentic blissfulness on her face. We drank wine. And I suddenly noticed that over the course of this entire time we didn't speak much. I was surprised that this didn't hamper us at all. Add to that the fact that we didn't introduce ourselves, didn't give our names, as though that didn't mean anything! And I also really liked that, it seemed unusual.

In the end, what's the difference? A wonderful evening, soft light, the green velvet of the tablecloths, a wonderful girl without a name across from me.... Unconstrained communication without discussion of what was next. I found out that she was studying to be "an artist," that she paints well, and loves chocolate. I liked her even more further. I left the question about her companion for later, it would have been out of place here.

At the end of the evening I already understood that it wasn't worth it for me to use this girl, and I needed to go to Tenetska through a different path.

When I walked her home to the entryway of her place, the strangest thing happened. She drew herself to me and kissed me on the cheek....

"Thank you. I had a really good time. When your keys clanged at my feet, I thought – just don't laugh! – that it was a heavenly bell.... She was silent for a bit, and then decisively uttered the unexpected: "If you'd marry me, I'd feel like the happiest woman in the world!

Strange, those candid words sent my thoughts in another direction – and why not?... What else am I waiting for from life? Why am I working, making up all this teleraving? Who needs me? Finally, when all this comes to a conclusion, will it be cheerful for me to look at the lonely walls of my building? And: not a single woman has spoken with me this way – they've all been waiting for the initiative from me, they were naughty, flirted, demanded, sometimes – threatened.... Tedium....

"Don't think that I'm a cretin," she continued. "I just KNOW that it has to be that way. How I know – I don't know...." She smiled: "Things like that happen with me. Here, for example, I know that you have two lighters in your pocket and...," she got lost in thought, seriously gazing into my eyes, "And a handkerchief – from yesterday, with bits of tobacco...."

As though bewitched, I rummaged in my pockets. One lighter was in my jeans, that I knew for sure. From the inner pocket of my sport coat I pulled out one more – an old, damaged one. I had nothing to say about the handkerchief. Everything was as she said.

"There, you see!" She was overjoyed.

"Nothing can be done," I laughed, "as a decent person I have to get married!"

"And are you a decent person?"

She had driven me into a dead end. I grew pensive:

"To be frank, I don't know...."

She was strange. I even became frightened for her future: will she be so straightforward and open with everyone?

"That means, decent...," she pecked at the sand with the toe of her sneaker the way children do. "That's it, thank you. I'll be going...."

But I couldn't just let her go! My curiosity smacked me in the head:

"No, stop! Do you have some more time?"

"Of course!!"

"Then let's go!"

I grabbed her by the hand again, and we jumped into the street and caught a ride with a car. She didn't ask about anything.

What happened further, I recall, was like a mirage. We went to one artist's place, my old friend. On the roof of his studio we drank champagne, vodka and Buratino brand citrus flavored water. Then together we went to yet one more studio and ended up at (it didn't seem strange to me) a grandiose banquet with *shashlik*, that was grilled in a courtyard in the middle of the city. My amazing little "frog princess" made an unsurpassed impression on the old wordsmiths and brushsmiths.

"You, old man, always get your share of the best," the owner of the studio endlessly stressed, tossing intense gazes in the direction of my wonderful unknown woman. "Look, she has the face of the Virgin Mary. And her skin! Look at her temple – Chinese porcelain. It's as if it's beaming! I also watchfully gazed at the "frog princess" and saw her eyes that were too large on her overly pale face and sensual lips that smiled the entire time, as everyone was indulging her in turn. This truly looked silly. I sat in the corner and followed all of this. I found nothing in her other than a captivating naturalness.

We sang, drank, and in the morning shot from an air rifle into the damp sky until the neighbors called the police. We had to brandish our ID cards and quickly dissolve in the milky rose-colored morning.

"Are you tired?" I asked her on the way.

"Of course not!" She was elated and fresh like the day that I saw her for the first time.

"Did you like all this mess?"

"A lot!"

I squeezed her hand: "Then I really need to get married…."

We stepped out of the car near her building.

"When?" She asked me seriously.

"Tomorrow if you like! Get ready – we'll go sign the marriage license paperwork!" I blurted out.

"Then – till tomorrow?"

"Till tomorrow!"

She was already standing at the doorway when it finally struck me that I didn't even know her name – I introduced her to everyone as "Princess" (in my mind adding – "frog")….

"What's your name, my fiancée?" I shouted with my intoxicated voice. She looked back.

"Lika."

"Anzhelika?" I inquired, and just barely failed to add – the "marquise of angels."

"Under no circumstances! Just – Lika. And no other way!

ELYZAVETA TENETSKA

1.

…Lately she all the more often recalled Vysotsky's song – "No, Guys, It's All Wrong!" Why it's "wrong," when here it is, happiness – recognition, realization of dreams, a home, a family. She lived to see it. Here she's driving a black and gray Opel to her three-room apartment in the center of town… And when she goes to any public place, she always hears whispering behind her back – either admiring or jealous, it doesn't matter. Why does that scent of mustiness all the more often follow her? It falls from the bottles of expensive perfume, reeks from the artists' canvases that hang in her apartment on the walls, from gifts that are sent to her from all quarters. From her very self. She already doesn't know whether she's really needed by anyone, or if all her friendly relations maintain mutually advantageous conditions: "you scratch my back, and I'll scratch yours." She doesn't know if she really has not lost her abilities, or if the recognition of her talent – is a tribute to the high position of her husband. Once she decided to verify this, she secretly drove to Lithuania where with a hidden camera she filmed the unique shots of the storming of the TV center and interviewed a bunch of people. But she didn't do it for fame. Next to the fires she was again truly happy. Because here at home, something "wasn't right." She was afraid of accepting the fact that she had deceived herself, that her expectations turned out to be vain. This was more horrifying to think about the fact that her husband wasn't a hero, but that he simply and almost accidentally ended up "under the iron fist" of authorities….

When he returns, she thought, and when he'll be lying alone, abandoned by everyone, covered in scabies, amid the icy wasteland – she'll go to lie next to him, giving him all her warmth. She was ready to freeze to death next to him, with him – silently and devotedly, like a dog. But that wasn't necessary. He returned. With a surprised and at the same time indifferent look he measured his daughter, drove Liza to his parents, quickly in a businesslike way "legalized relations" and dove into politics. And only because, Liza suspected, there was no other path for him – the same way there was no other path for the Communist Youth League workers who plunged into business, he became a politician.

For three or four years he would come home just in the wee hours of the morning, most often he reeked of alcohol. At first – the cheap stuff, then the expensive. He professionally learned to make speeches, his articles, photos and biographical blurbs more often began to appear on the pages of the press. And Liza noticed that this gave him satisfaction. If over the course of two or three weeks there wasn't a word about him on TV or in the newspapers, he grew tarnished, like a copper kopeck in water, and thought up methods for reminding them about his existence. It surprised Liza that he didn't go over to the opposition, but, as they wrote in the press – "he distinguished himself by his tolerance," which for Liza, to tell the truth, more resembled adjustment. In younger days she listened with delight to his "kitchen" speeches, she was sure that he was passionate, but now his rehearsals in front of the mirror irritated her, his meetings with image makers, his bodyguards. But most disgusting was the fact that she took advantage of the blessings, that unexpectedly fell on her head. But now, when her husband could sponsor her projects, they became uninteresting for her….

Everything that provoked ecstasy and euphoria at first now oppressed her. Slowly the most honest voices grew quiet, but the SYSTEM continued its existence. It reminded Liza of an hourglass: you turn it upside down – and it sprinkles again, just in the opposite direction… And Liza decided to swim with the flow. Now she wanted just one thing – to ensure a normal life for her child.

Lika grew up a little bit strange – she was too quiet, too deeply inside herself. At seven she painted and hung up in her room a banner with a drawing and a sign, made with her funny children's handwriting: "People, you are free!" And her contented father often took his comrades in arms to the child's room until the girl tore down the banner from the wall. She could paint for hours, and Liza put her in a special school for artists, and after that – in the Institute, where she immediately became an "odd bird… ."[16]

Thank God, she didn't do drugs and didn't hang out at discos. But Liza didn't know what to expect from her in the future.

---

16 Literally "bila vorona" means a "white crow," someone who sticks out or doesn't fit in.

2.

The news was stunning: Lika was getting married. Liza was sure that her daughter had no suitors, and suddenly such a surprise! Add to that, as it became clear, she didn't even know the last name of her future husband – just his first name and where he worked. Liza had to immediately get on the phone. She sighed with relief just when, through her friends, she found out that Denys Volodymyrovych Severyn – was a well-to-do, respectable person with prospects; additionally, he was a colleague. He graduated from the same institute as she, and now was successfully working in the advertising business. So he wasn't hunting after either money or the prestige of the bride-to-be's father.

"Do you at least understand that it's not done like this?" Liza asked.

"You'll see everything yourself," Lika answered in a whisper. "You can't help but understand… I knew that HE has to be exactly like this.

"When will we see him?"

"I don't know. I've been thinking about that myself. It seems to me that he won't want to go right away to meet the parents. He's serious and mature. I would just go to him and that'd be it…."

"Have we pestered you so much?"

"No, but I don't want any kind of wedding. It doesn't matter to me. I never even expected that this could happen: it happens – and everything is changing abruptly! It's all the same to me where we'll live. I'm ready to go with him wherever he goes – to any remote corner."

"I'm sure that he won't take you to some remote corner," Liza smiled. "But you have to show him to your father."

"Daddy won't like him…."

"Why do you think so?"

"He's completely different. He's a "drummer.""

"What do you mean? Does he play in a group?"

"No, a "drummer" is someone who doesn't give a "ratatatat" about anything. He said that himself.

"Hardly… I've been told he's a business person…."

"I hate that word! You see, you can work and even achieve something, but with all that you can remain a "drummer." That's advanced aerobatics.

"No, I don't understand. So, he doesn't give a "ratatatat" about you?"

"Maybe," Lika calmly agreed. "But that's just for the time being. I know that he'll love me. For a long-long time. You'll see…."

"God let it be… We'll see."

The time for getting acquainted happened the next day in the evening. In the morning an application was given to the Marriage Registration Office, and after classes at the institute Lika phoned and announced that she was bringing her "fiancé" home….

3.

Her husband was delayed as always. Liza phoned him on his cell and each time heard the same thing: "I'll be there in ten minutes!" She had to meet the visitor herself. He entered following Lika, and Elyzaveta cast a severe glance at him. Several important questions worried her: was he a druggie, or "gay" (there was enough of that on TV), or was he a skirt chaser?

But from the first glance it was clear that he was nothing of the kind, she could really like someone like him. The visitor was tall, fit, with a rather interesting face, light hair that was gathered on the nape of his neck in a neat "tail," and with a stylish "three-day" stubble on his cheekbones. Jeans, a sweater… For some reason he looked like a sailor who recently had just stepped on the shore. At any rate, his look was a bit wild and a little sullen, as though he were looking at the world for the first time.

Liza was a bit shocked from the sudden thought that this stranger will be touching her child.

"This – is Denys," Lika said, helping her guest hang his jacket. Liza smiled her official smile and extended her hand. A diamond flashed like the flash of a camera onto her finger in the light of a dark faint light in the entrance hall. His movements were unsure.

Liza set the table in the living room. True, at the request of Lika, everything was simple: a bottle of French cognac from her father's reserves, cookies, grapes. The conversation was strained. Earlier Liza would have been distressed about it, but not now. She didn't want to be like a mother hen who interrogates her son-in-law about his wealth, past life and housing situation. Liza turned on the sconce lighting – in this kind of calm illumination she felt more assured – and while the visitor was pouring out a drink, she pushed a large crystal ashtray toward herself, started to smoke and leaned back against the tall back of the armchair.

"Now here," Lika smiled. "Now – be wary! When a guest comes to us and mama sits like this – it means that the "x-ray has been turned on"… My mama – is a witch!"

"What kind of nonsense are you talking?! Well then, let's drink to our acquaintance!" Liza took a small glass that her guest had extended to her.

They sat for just a little bit. Then Lika accompanied her guest to the elevator.

4.

"Do you reckon this is the biggest stupidity of your life?" Lika asked when they were standing on the stairway platform.

In answer he pressed her to himself and kissed her on the nose – like a child.

"Something wrong?" She continued to pump him. "Have you changed your mind?"

"No," he answered after a pause, "no…."

"Did mama frighten you? Don't worry, she's always that way, a lot of people are wary of her, especially daddy's guests. But she liked you. I understood that right away."

Perplexed, he moved his shoulders and pressed the elevator call button. When he had already entered the elevator and the doors gently closed, Lika pressed up to them with her face:

"You're going to love me for a long time…," she whispered to the closed space, "I know…."

DENYS

1.

That morning I wanted to put on a suit, but I remembered that yesterday I had spilled coffee on my slacks, and my other suit was too official. So I slipped into my jeans and sweater. I strove not to grow pensive over what I was planning to do. I didn't even inform my parents about my "fate-bearing decision," though, I know, my mother would be joyful. It's no big deal. I'll tell her later. Though I don't know whether my "frog princess" was kidding, or whether we both simply had gone mad. Let all be that will be. Maybe the sign of fate is in this: through Liza a wondrous sweet girl had come to me, who unexpectedly had decided to become my wife. Poor girl doesn't yet know that I'm an egotist and cynic. But with her appearance everything has to change – those languid visions, and my meaningless earning of money, attacks of boredom and superficial relations with women.

I didn't go to work. I waited for Lika in the café till eleven, drank coffee and mindlessly flipped through the newspapers. Then she arrived. From far away I didn't even recognize her – she was in a short, fluffy sheepskin coat, with a different hairdo. In her hands she was holding a bouquet of pink roses. I was perplexed because, clod that I am, I didn't think about buying at least one flower! We drove over to the Marriage Registration Office (B-r-r-r!), and then to her place. Shame was strangling me. I said that to her. I can't stand any contacts with bureaucrats. I wish we could have avoided all this. I was indifferent as to who her parents were, how they would react to the sudden wedding of their daughter. It didn't concern me. She agreed and was ready just to move to my place right away, but I looked at her delicate profile and wide open green eyes and decided that I needed to go through this unpleasant procedure to the end. Because, as intuition prompted, the girl was from a wealthy family. And in wealthy families everything is decided at the supper table….

…Not only couldn't I tell her parents about my achievements and future prospects – what I was, in fact, planning to chat with them about – I couldn't breathe. It was as though from within I instantly was covered with wooden scabs, and each chip was jammed into my lungs. This was… horror, an apparition, the grin of fate, the blow from the butt-end of an axe, devilry, absurd, idiocy, hanky-panky, the end to everything, death: Liza came out to meet me from the dim light of the entryway.

Right then when I was ready to make a decisive step back away from my troublesome memories, it turned out – I made my way toward them! And in what way! Is it worth saying that I was again blinded and struck dumb. I noticed her ring flash in front of me. I bowed and carelessly ended up with my lips on the little cold stone. And this completely knocked me off the tracks. Once again I turned into an eighteen-year-old moron, quaking with sexual desire, impatience and feeling hopeless. I don't remember how I sat through at meet-the-fiancé show, all my efforts were reduced to stopping my shaking, speaking in an even-pitched voice, and not letting her recognize me. At a certain moment of this horrible engagement ritual I realized the wedding wouldn't happen, that I needed to immediately get up and go. I was almost ready to do that. But something kept me back. We sat there for just a short time. I used a pressing business meeting as an excuse and I quickly retreated. I needed to deliberate on how to do it so I wouldn't insult Lika. She went out with me to the elevator. It was curious: when we were left alone, it was as if I had regained my sight. Lika stood before me like the incarnation of a holiday – her eyes were radiant. What should I have said? "Thank you, little one, the practical joke has been successful?.." But, looking at her, I understood that she would simply die. I don't know why such certitude cropped up in me. She'll die. Or… or the same thing will befall her as did me. And I well knew what that was. I kissed her, desiring just one thing – that the elevator would come as quickly as possible.

2.

Of course I didn't go to a meeting. I dropped by at Suok – a little restaurant that elicited touching childhood memories for me. It was made in the form of a circus tent, the walls were adorned with paintings from the first illustrated edition of *Three Fat Men* – the gymnast Tibul in a mask and black tricot, the doctor Gaspar Arneri with a test tube in his hand, the comic teacher of dance Razdvatrys[17] with a delicately-pink porcelain doll under his arm and, of course, a little girl with the strange name Suok, who was balancing on a ball. I sat across from the painting, ordered a vodka and fixed my eyes on the azure-gray painting. After the third shot (with no snacks), the little girl on the ball seemed to me to be three-dimensional, and the expression of her face – alive. She had reddish curls and green eyes, she was laughing. After the fifth shot I understood whom she reminded me of. Lika….

I suddenly thought that all the same I'd love her. She was dealt to me like a card – then and now. I already loved her when I found out that Liza had a child. Undoubtedly! I'd love her in any case, and from that, maybe, you can't hide. So, it had to be so! I'll love and look after her. In

---

17   Meaning: "Onetwothree."

addition, if Liza existed in my life like a phantom – now I got close to her in reality. This is something different than resorting to fantasies. Maybe this will give me the ability to overcome them, to calm down. Besides that, I understood that she didn't recognize me.

Having thought about Liza, I already couldn't stop. She nearly hadn't changed at all. Even more so, she was one of those women to whom age just adds to their charm. Yes, her features sharpened and from that more expressively the essence of her character was reflected on her face – bright, unique, quite cruel, and eternally captivating. Medea, the Medusa Gorgon, the Shullamite could have had that kind of face. Every line of the Song of Songs fit her. I tried to remember that they spoke about "honey and milk beneath your tongue" and the same kind of trembling enveloped me. Yes, she didn't recognize me. I was just an episode in her life. It's too bad that the same didn't happen with me….

…Suok came off the wall and sat down opposite me, she doubled in my eyes, from which her lips seemed smeared, and her eyes – slanted and cunning.

"Are we feeling lonesome or sad?" Suok asked.

"We're drinking," I answered, pushing a second glass toward her and filling it.

Suok downed it almost in a single gulp and leaned back on the chair, stretching out her legs in black fishnet stockings. I reached out to offer her cigarettes and clicked the lighter.

"Will we be friends?" Suok asked. "Do you have money?"

I slapped my pocket.

"Wonderful!" Suok was overjoyed. "Do you like me?"

"I don't know… What's the difference?..."

"Really, none!" Suok was even more overjoyed. "But I like you. Right away you can see – you're a decent man. Just don't drink anymore. Otherwise nothing will come of it."

"Nothing comes of it anyway," I waved her away from me.

"Are you impotent?" Suok clapped her hands together.

"Why are you asking?" I couldn't understand.

"Ah… Then everything is okay. With whom does it work out these days? That's just crap! Here you are, such a cool man, and you're sitting all by your lonesome, all sad, drinking vodka. Boredom! What do you need?"

Yes, I had enough of everything. I had an interesting job, a nice apartment, healthy parents, students who adored me, women, who were ready to come over when I call, a not very burdensome solitude – a full past. Now everything could acquire even more distinction – I'll have a wife, children, and I, most likely, would get fish for an aquarium and a dog. I looked at Suok.

"I have everything. But it's as if everything's not mine…."

"I didn't understand!" Suok got closer, set her elbows on the table and stared at me with her doubled eyes.

"Well… It happens like that: life gives you an error at the very beginning. It's like computers – you press the wrong key and everything crumples, turns into incomprehensible symbols.

"It seems I understand you," Suok grew pensive. "It was like that with me. I call these situations "Only if…."

"That is?"

"Lord! Well, here's an example for you: if I hadn't been fucked in the eighth grade, right now I'd be… let's say, sitting in your office and powdering the brains of your businessmen. Do you have that kind of job?…"

"More or less."

"There, you see! And how many of those "ifs" do each of us have! So what should you do now – die?!"

She was right. Her smeared lips proclaimed the truth, she seemed like a good fairy who had come off her peeling magical bubble to me. We left the restaurant together. I didn't want to take her to my place, so I took a hotel room. In the middle of the night when she was sleeping, I quietly went away, leaving money on the bed. It wasn't Suok.

I understood that from that moment fate had tossed me yet one more "if only...," but it, more than anything, concerned Lika: if the day before yesterday I hadn't wandered after her...."

LIKA
LIKA'S FIRST MONOLOGUE

"A wedding and a funeral – here are two performances at which the "culprits of the action" don't play any role. It's collective labor, a ritual, where it's impossible to think about the essential meaning of these rites. What does the aroused throng have to do with the couple that is sitting at the table at the place of honor and periodically clutching at the signal of the shout of "Kiss now!"[18] This is just a command to drink... It's so good we avoided that!"

" ...?"

"A funeral? Imagine how hard it is when they look at you like at a doll... And you aren't capable of stirring or expressing a protest against this contemplation. Does the understanding of loss approach then? A funeral – that's also collective work when the tables are set, when the potatoes are peeled – in buckets (!) and you make boiled dumplings. Who thought all this up? Death and love – two mysteries, in which there is no room for strangers!"

" ...!"

"Of course, my love! And you fancied that I'm a little girl, who never read anything more complex than the fairytales of Charles Perro? You can't even imagine what universe is swirling in my head. Sometimes I'm even

____

18 "Hirko" literally means "it's bitter." In the Ukrainian tradition, everyone shouts that while raising a glass in toast to the newlyweds so they can sweeten it with a kiss.

90

terrified. That's why I'm so happy that you are with me, that I found you and you will save me...."

"...?"

"From everything, from the terrifying... You know, there are people over whom – it's uncertain why and on which merits – at a certain moment the sky opens up. Don't you understand? I'll try to explain it – I haven't talked about this with anyone. I've been waiting for you. One time – I was two years old at the time – I was sitting on the floor of our little room (we were living in a communal apartment) and I tried to paint something. The light was falling in a way that everything to me seemed too bright, like in Impressionist paintings (of course back then I didn't know that they existed!): a red wooden floor (then it was painted and shone in the sun like ice), orange flowers on the shades, bright walls (mother always loved pure colors). In a wide and direct ray of the twilight sun golden ballerinas danced... I tried to paint all of this when it started to grow dark in the room and I looked around. Mama was standing in the doorway and looking at me. I couldn't see her well because she was standing opposite the light – just the silver contour of her elongated body... What's wrong, my love? Of course, smoke! So. This was a picture taken from life. But right then it was as if I suddenly heard music. Don't laugh! It happens like that in childhood. That picture till this day stands before my eyes. It was right then that I sensed invisible feathers being strewn at me and enveloping me in warmth. To this day I'm surprised how vividly and simply a child can feel the touch of God. That moment, when we were looking at one another, a strange feeling grew ripe in me, that time is – fleeting. Right now I can express it, but then I was warm and fearful. I precisely sensed that everything around me and with every moment I was turning into a... memory. Simply – into someone's memory."

"...?"

"People from birth and to that moment when they begin to understand the inevitability of their passing – slowly turn into a cocoon of memories for other people. Those who have the biggest cocoon, are happy people, there aren't very many of them. I looked at mama and physically sensed her becoming a memory for me, so that moments emerged and each was different from the next. With time we absorb each other even more despairingly, as though we're thirty, because we begin to understand that not a single moment will be repeated. You know that with this very same sensation I used to kiss my grandmother's hands… I always kissed her – simply pecked her on the cheek, and one time took her hands into mine – they were warm, in bluish veins and in a net of wrinkles, with thin parchment skin – and I kissed her because I suddenly understood: she'll be gone soon! It was so terrifying for me. If only everyone could understand this – would we cause pain to each other? Would we talk so much, so complicatedly and so… unnecessarily? Words, like tobacco smoke, that beclouds memories…."

LIKA'S SECOND MONOLOGUE

"If people only could see – like in the movies! – the movements of the soul, they could better understand actions that happen in their own life."

"…?"

"Right now I'll recount one of Chekhov's stories…."

"…!"

"Well, don't laugh, I didn't express that right! I'll retell it to you as though I'm recounting it anew. Do you understand? It's very similar to all this life. I read it so long ago that I already don't remember the title… Now then. A doctor's little son dies. The doctor is inconsolable. It seems to him that his life has ended with the loss of his son. Suddenly – a ring at the door. A man comes and begs the doctor to immediately go with him to his seriously ill wife, whom he loves madly. The doctor at first refuses – he's incapable of moving from his spot. But, in the end, obligation takes over, and he rides off in the night to the home of the patient. They go to the apartment. But here it turns out that his wife's illness is her way of conniving to send away her betrayed husband from the house so she can run away with some military man. Her husband is in despair. Forgetting about the doctor, he runs through the rooms, jostles against things that are strewn about, and can't understand anything. He's outraged, crushed, disgraced. The doctor, in his turn, doesn't understand anything: he has his own misfortune, he's abandoned everything, has driven God knows where – and suddenly before him some guy is scurrying about, appealing for justice. Here they should have cried together, shaken each other's hands, empathized with each other – for both of them were in pain! But no! They argue, accuse each other of who knows what. Each one's own outrage is screaming. It seems to me that this story presents the model of all human relations."

"…?"

"Here, for example, that salesgirl, from whom we bought a melon… Do you remember, you even got angry when I talked to her? But is that her fault that we're happy, and she's in a dirty apron?! Our happiness was intolerable for her – and she overcharged us. But I had pity for her, because at home in the evening her drunken husband is waiting for her – and she doesn't get a single kiss!"

"…."

"There are simple truths – people don't often speak about them, and if they speak, then, usually, they do so ironically. Or maybe they sound too banal. But they do exist. Try expressing them out loud – and you'll feel tears rolling: you need to love your friends, defend your homeland, respect the elderly, not belittle those weaker than you, not lie, fear nothing, and ask for nothing… It's maybe funny to talk about this. But… we don't laugh when we read the Bible…."

Irene Rozdobudko

LIKA'S THIRD MONOLOGUE

"Before meeting you my own helplessness weighed me down. I was told that I paint well, and I almost believed it. But then I understood: if you can't be a GREAT artist – it's better not to be one at all! You can be consoled by the fact that you're doing something 'for yourself.' But I find it ridiculous! I always paint for myself and anywhere I might be. And for a certain moment a painting brings me relief. Is this egotism? The more so – right now."

"…"

"No, I won't stop painting. That's impossible. Over myself I sense a certain substance that thirsts to express itself through me. I just don't know why precisely through me… Maybe that is MY substance, something in the form of a spirit close to me that wanders in the noosphere. How hard it is to sense it and not have the ability to help with something! It approximately appears like this: something from above speaks to me, as though through a thick wadded layer, I try to understand, hear it, but the words get lost, I hear just the end, unintelligible sounds, and I can't transform them into a painting! But THERE they're waiting precisely for my word, but I am – silent… Horror. And from this my silence, first and foremost my substance, betrayed by me, suffers. Maybe in order to express yourself – you need to be free. Free, from everything. But that's impossible…."

"…."

"Freedom – is the possibility of being yourself, everywhere and always. And when people believe in you, regardless of your earnings, status or way you dress. Regarding everything external. Freedom – is taking as much as possible on yourself – ten times more than you can bear. You'll be out of breath, bend, but at a certain moment you'll sense that there is no load: it's 'taken, ' you're free – in word, in your mode of life, in love… You'll learn to understand more than others."

LIKA'S FOURTH MONOLOGUE

"Only a person is capable of lying. There is no lying amid nature. Do the trees, birds and water lie? I always sense a lie, like an animal – with all my skin, with everything that's inside me – from my stomach to my soul. You can live needy, senselessly, stupidly, thoughtlessly, with difficulty, but with all this you have to live honestly! Otherwise it's – gloom, night, death… The most horrifying is to lose your faith. You lose it once – it's forever… And then you search. And you find justification for yourself. You make believe that everything is okay and smile. But a needle remains in your heart. You can live with it somehow. But is that life?"

DENYS

1.

…I openly envy people who look at the world with eyes wide open. Everything surprises them, everything arouses their ecstatic rapture. I have long had no trust in the world. The historical streets of Europe washed with a special shampoo would look much better to me in their original appearance – with the scent of sewage poured out of windows, and with the fumes of the end products of human activities.

The world has become too phoney. Fake "Potemkin villages" are nothing compared to the scope of this sham. In Egypt – in this mysterious country that the waves of time have engulfed – in the evening, sitting outside a certain amount of time near their tents, zealous "Bedouins" put on their clothes, wrap their heads in *keffiyehs*, and rush in their jeeps into the heart of the desert to put on a performance from the lives of their ancient ancestors in front of their bewildered audience; in Finland, celebrating the anniversary of Sibelius, gray-haired elderly women put on pathetic full skirts made of rustling taffeta and striped stockings in order to perform chorales in front of the monument to the composer – and all this for these same tourists....

I've traveled a great deal in recent years, and more and more often with melancholy I recall the mountains and forests of Western Ukraine. What's there now? Can it be true that "ecotourism" has turned them into the very same theater, and abandoned wooden huts are now just a decoration?

No matter what, I've always loved everything natural. Rubber-skinned beauties produced by the efforts of the cosmetic industry have never attracted me. Genuineness has been preserved in the wrinkles of the elderly and the touching dimples of infants. And that naturalness was in Lika. She no longer intimidated me as when I first met her. What upset me was that after we met, she abandoned her studies before even entering the last year of school. Time and again I asked her to get readmitted to the institute, but she responded to that with a slight shrug of her shoulders and an uncertain half-smile. She lived like a bird, a sparrow that would chirp joyfully one moment and then would sit frowning the next, completely indifferent to what it would eat tomorrow. To be honest, it was good enough for me.

During the first months of our odd marriage I was struck with horror by what had happened. Besides, I realized that I wasn't equipped for family life. I couldn't come home on time. I didn't know how to plan our weekends and buy the things we needed. I had no intention of forsaking my old habits. And I hated giving an account of all my movements around the city. Once I even turned nasty to Lika and couldn't understand how she had managed to put those fetters on me. For half a year straight I would come home at midnight and not always sober. Even when I WANTED to go to her, I forced myself to turn to Suok or to go to the sauna, or I would even spend a night in someone's studio. This unseemly behavior lasted till I suddenly realized: all this was unnecessary! After all, in no way did Lika protest against my displays of freedom and independence, she never treated them as a rebellion, and, I think, she didn't even understand their implication. So what would I dispute?!

Never once did she reproach me or ask me where I was and with whom.

I calmed down without even noticing it and realized that it wasn't a game, or chains, or a trap....

2.

"A desperate tenderness " – that's how one could characterize my feelings toward Lika. "Despair and tenderness" would be even more precise, but it sounded too hopeless. It seemed that she locked herself up within four walls with such a bastard like me by mistake. I used to buy her plenty of various things for painting, I used to get her expensive oil colors, canvases, pencils, sketch box easels – large and portable. I really liked her paintings a lot. Yet I felt she was painting only to make me happy – and for no other reason. On a few occasions I suggested that she should arrange an exhibition, but in response to it she repeated her favorite gesture – she shrugged her shoulders insecurely. At times it irritated me, maybe because I myself couldn't escape from vanities in that way. But she could live on bare branches with such comfort and calm.

When she didn't paint, she sewed. Rather, she had an exquisite skill for remaking something ordinary into small masterpieces. All her things were original. I especially remember her jeans jacket that she ornamented with special paints and onto which she sewed fabric-covered buttons; on their fabric, in some peculiar way, she painted miniature images of angels. At one of the parties, one highly esteemed woman offered an incredible sum of money for this work of art, and after that she annoyingly kept calling, begging Lika to make something similar for her. The jacket deeply touched me. I loved seeing her wear it, I'd buckle these amazing buttons with particular tenderness.

However, Lika didn't like it when I treated her like a child. In fact, she was not a child; at times she looked at me in a way that made me uncomfortable. I tried to ignore looks like that, I tried to dismiss the thought that Lika was an abyss into which a man could fall. I called her endearing names on purpose, realizing that I did it in order not to fall, not to give way to my feelings, which would be unlike those of a father, lenient and disparaging.

3.

We were at her parents' place no more than six or seven times over the course of a year at various family gatherings. More often we ran into them at various official parties, private showings or presentations that I was forced to attend from time to time. A day or two before the scheduled event I would be so sick that I'd drink myself blind, I tried to come back home as late as possible, when Lika was asleep, and I would stay in the kitchen smoking all night long, making excuses like "problems at work." That's why I looked fairly worn-out during their every visit – with black circles under my eyes and bristles on my sunken cheekbones. And then Lika's parents gave her sympathetic looks, and I would protest my presence at that patriarchal-family table. After all, it was easier for me that way. I was sort of dozing, squinting my eyes and behaving somewhat sluggishly just like a real recluse. Of course, all of that was make-believe and play. It was easier that way for me to conceal my insatiable curiosity and to quench the storm of emotions boiling up in me. My voracious interest verged on a fetish. In the bathroom, like a complete idiot, I checked through HER shampoos and creams, twisted HER toothbrush and dipped my face in HER towel, restraining myself from digging in a linen basket. I dreamt about seeing her one day wearing her robe and slippers on her bare feet, and that one thought made me feel giddy. Of course, another feeling added to all that horror – that I was a scoundrel. Nonetheless, I kept watching her. With a phoney indifference I listened avidly to everything she said, trying to understand what made her life, what her thoughts and desires were. And she required just one thing from me – she wanted me to be a good husband for Lika. Yet the entire appearance I was assuming two days before the visit was eloquently telling a different story. And, as usual, she kept ignoring me, throwing sympathetic glances at her daughter, as though saying: "Well, I warned you...."

Her husband, my father-in-law, dumbfounded me, if not to say more. When I first met him, I felt confused and at a loss. Yes, he did have a presentable appearance and was very eloquent, but his good physical condition and youthfulness were as false as everything he said. At that point he crossed over to a different camp once and for all and became an active proponent of the old days. The moment I carelessly remarked that in those "wonderful days" he was cleaning shit holes, he cut loose an outraged diatribe against the nouveau riche, brainwashed by money and power, and refuses to notice all the shamefulness of his current well-being. And I was ostentatiously spreading red caviar on a slice of bread – two layers! – under Lika's ironic gaze. That was the end of my communication with my father-in-law. He tried to avoid me, and most often Liza received us alone. But it was even more difficult. We were not getting any closer (it was out of the question!), and I continued to be a bad son-in-law in her eyes. It was obvious. And only Lika, as always, was beaming with happiness, chuckling occasionally into her fist. Everything that was going on outside her parents' home was good enough for her.

4.

We went back home, two or three days passed, and everything settled down. I went to work, Lika waited for me at home, nicely setting the table for dinner. I liked that. I was turning into a philistine. More likely, I had always been one. At one point I wanted more comfort. Yes, I wanted it, not Lika. At that time (and I still remember it with horror and despair) a wardrobe caught my eye....

I had never cared that much about making my home more comfortable, but once, when Lika and I were taking a walk along a railway station square, I noticed a sign of a new furniture store, and my glance glided over a glass shop window. A very original "edifice" stood there in splendor - almost a room made of oak with carved patterns and all kinds of knobs.

"Take a look," I said, "that's whom I would address with the formal "vy." Do you remember the line in your favorite Chekhov: 'Esteemed wardrobe....'"[19]

Lika laughed.

"This is no wardrobe," I continued, "this is a true 'Nest of Gentlefolk!'[20] one can live in it!"

"Can we afford to buy it?" Lika, who did not take much interest in the financial standing of our family, asked.

"No, we should buy it! Let's go!"

We entered the store and it turned out it was a display, one-of-a-kind. It was there to test consumer demand. It made Lika sad it wasn't for sale.

"And when will you test the demand for it?"

"In a month or two. No sooner than that," the salesman answered, "and then we'll start taking orders."

"Oh, that's a shame!" Lika flung her arms up in frustration.

I calmed her down all the way back home.

"But this is the only thing that you wanted to buy in all this time!" She couldn't let it go. "I just hope all your wishes would always come true!"

"To hell with it, with this wooden box!"

I started to regret dragging her to the store. She took everything too seriously. I had to think of something else fast, and in the next store I my eye caught some luxurious,

---

19 From Chekhov's short story "The Shooting Party. " "Shkaf" can be also be translated as cupboard or cabinet.

20 The title of Turgenev's novel published in 1859.

though quite gaudy, bed sheets. Then we bought a standing lamp and antique writing utensils. It all made no sense at all, but it created the atmosphere of a joint family thing.

"Do you really like all this?" Lika kept asking, dubiously examining our purchases when we came back home.

"Not really...."

"Let's give it away to people then...."

"What people?"

"Any people. To those who would really need it."

"Great! Considering that the cheapest thing of all this stuff costs more than a hundred bucks!" I couldn't help saying it. And I couldn't control myself further: "Do you enjoy living like this? Being a home kitten when you are smart and talented?! Sometimes when you serve me like in a hotel, I feel like a complete moron! Is that interesting for you? No, of course, as a regular guy I am just fine with this state of things – 'good home and a wife by my side. What else does one need to meet old age with dignity....' But I feel like some kind of a tyrant. Is it the life you wanted? Is it interesting for you?"

I kicked at the standing lamp with my foot. She got embarrassed. I got scared.

"Listen," I said in a calmer voice, "I didn't want to insult you. I just feel sorry that you are wasting your time and... life. "

"Love is never worthless. I don't understand you.... "

It seemed she really didn't understand. And I ceased any attempt to have any influence on her ambition.

In about a month and a half she received a call from the institute. They offered her to take part in an annual biennale that took place in a picturesque nook in the Carpathian mountains. I was happy that she was not forgotten. Lika wasn't very enthusiastic about going, but when our kitchen was overcrowded with her former fellow students and her former professor, her eyes sparkled. All of them, noisy and cheerful, glanced in my direction with misgiving. For no reason! I radiated good nature, poured out wine for them. And I showed with my entire expression that I was not going to stand in the way of a young talent. And that was true.

"Fine, I'll go," Lika said after all the guests had gone, "if all of you desire that so much...."

"Here it is again! You're doing it for somebody else's sake again! And you are a talented artist, it's your world, your surroundings. After all, you can sell your artwork there and.... Oh! I know! You'll sell your paintings and then buy me a wardrobe as a gift!"

She needed a push, an idea for the sake of which she could tear herself away from this cosy home existence. And she liked my idea. She even clapped her hands and started to pack her painter's paraphernalia right away even though there was still a week before the biennale.

This artistic event looked something like this: somewhere at the foot of a mountain a small "art town" was set up. Tents were put up for the participants, and a place for an improvised private showing area was constructed under a huge canvas tent. For two weeks in a row talented young people worked in the open air, putting up their old and new pieces for sale. From time to time journalists, TV reporters, art critics, and foreign collectors were brought there by buses.

"It will be crazy," Lika explained to me, partying all night long. Forget about painting! Profanation, that's all...."

"You're exaggerating. And if you don't like it there, at least you'll have a chance to be outdoors, to breathe some fresh air and just take a break from me, a fool.... And I'll come to visit you. And we'll be walking in the mountains!"

This thought gave me the chills and I fell silent....

5.

I love September. This year it was particularly warm and somehow delicious – toward evening, the air, filled with the scent of coffee, developed a rich leaf-like aroma with a touch of chrysanthemums. Lika was leaving early in the morning with the last group. A day earlier I arranged with the guys that they would take care of her stuff ahead of time, since on the day of departure I had so much important work to do that I wasn't able to see her off. So Lika didn't have to carry her heavy French easel by herself.

In the morning we had coffee and I tried to make her have at least a small bite of a sandwich, but she categorically refused to eat.

"Well, what's this all about?" I asked. "You'll take a few weeks break from home, from me.... Somebody else would look forward to it...."

"Don't ever say that – 'somebody else.' I don't know what other people would do, I hate to be without you. It's as if you'd be missing some important body part – an arm, for example, or a leg. Would you be able to walk without a leg?!"

"I'd buy crutches!" I smiled.

"You're joking. I mean it...."

I called for a cab. In the hallway I gently fastened my favorite buttons on her jacket.

"This angel adores you, this one will protect you, this one will keep you safe, and this one is a bit angry...." She said while I was busy with the clasps.

I was worried a bit, as though she, in fact, were a little child. But with each fastened button, a hardly perceptible tiny wave of joy rose inside me, I was glad she was leaving, that I'd have a chance to be alone, I'll TRY to be alone without her. Of course I wouldn't dare to say that out loud, it would hurt her.

Already on the threshold Lika wrapped her arms around my neck and stood still.

"You know what," I lost control of myself, "if you don't want to go – stay! It looks like I'm sending you to penal servitude. Heaven knows what!"

She took a step back and smiled:

"Okay, okay. I should go!"

"O, God," I remembered suddenly, "how about money?!"

I quickly went back to the room, grabbed a pile of money from a drawer and held it out to Lika.

"Why would I need so much?"

"Take it, just in case! What if you don't like it there – if that happens, you can stay at a hotel, or take a plane back home, after all."

She shoved the money into a pocket of her jeans and quickly closed the door behind her. From the window I watched her take the cab, and like an old woman, I made the sign of cross over her as she was leaving....

6.

I was left alone. I didn't feel any particular relief. I had some more coffee and started to get ready for a meeting. I acted almost mechanically. My thoughts worked in a different direction. I was left alone for the first time in two years. Maybe it was time to meet with Liza? But – what for? I had no intention of committing adultery! And still more and more I wanted to assert myself somehow, to remind her of what I never forgot, unlike her. Maybe even to punish her, make her suffocate with all the horror of the situation, just as I suffocated the moment she stepped out to us out of the darkness of her hallway. Yes, very much so. It would be worthwhile to put a big fat period to the end of this story in order to never again sit at their unctuous family table.

I quickly wrapped up the meeting, stopped by at the Suok restaurant, reenergized myself with two shots of cognac for courage, and dialed her cell phone number.

At first I reported that Lika had left, and gave a detailed account of what she was wearing and what she took with her, and answered a few more stupid questions. And then I suggested that we should meet for an "important talk." She was surprised.

"Fine.... Come to our place. I have two hours of free time.... "

Not at their place, I thought. An invitation to a restaurant would also seem weird.

"Is something wrong? What happened? Should I come over to your place?" Liza got worried.

We agreed that I'd take a cab and pick her up at an intersection in half an hour. She agreed. I still had some time to stop by at the nearest grocery store – I couldn't just treat her to yesterday's borscht! Only God knew what was going on in my head.... If I was going to toss all the darkness of my twenty-year hell onto her – why did I, like a true seducer, grab champagne, Martini,[21] and all kinds of colorful cans?! And if my aim was to achieve this very aim – what a scoundrel I would be in her eyes!..

I saw her from a distance and my heart jolted like a little ball tied to a rubber thread. She looked very elegant, as always. A clingy black dress (it may seem strange, but I didn't remember a different color on her, except for the white swimming suit she wore near the swimming pool ages ago), high heeled shoes, and sleek hair brushed back. She gave me a nod without the slightest hint of friendliness and sat in the front seat. I kept looking at a thin strand of hair that had loosened from an otherwise perfect hairstyle, greedily inhaling the aroma of her perfumes – the same ones: she never changed her taste in things that she liked.

"Liza, is that really you?" I felt like whispering to that austere nape of her neck. I've thought about you all my life. What should I do now? You tell me. I'll do whatever you say."

---

21   Martini & Rossi vermouth. Ukrainians call it Martini.

7.

We went up the elevator without uttering a word. I could feel her haughtiness with my skin, her indifference and unwillingness to look into the problems with which I dared waste her time.

I fumbled with the key for a while. I would have been even glad if it had broken. I was so embarrassed as if I were not thirty-eight ,but eighteen, as I was back then.... She came in, walked around the rooms the way a mistress of the house walks, and peeked at the kitchen, probably to assess the degree of comfort in the apartment. After Lika left, a certain disorder reigned, two cups were sitting on a table along with an unfinished sandwich.

"Here's something I bought...," I said guiltily and began to rustle with plastic bags, taking groceries and bottles out, "I'll make you coffee."

"You don't need to. I'm pressed for time," she said, while sitting down on a chair and getting a cigarette from her purse, "it's quite nice here. Can I take another walk around?"

"Of course."

I was glad she left me alone for a moment. I quickly took the cups away, threw out the sandwich, wiped the table clean, put everything I had bought on it, and turned on the coffee maker.

"It's a nice place," She noted when she came back, "to tell the truth, I didn't expect.... So what did you want to talk to me about? About Lika?"

A shudder passed over me as if someone had poured cold water down the back of my collar.

"No.... Would you like some Martini?" I offered, realizing that, with every minute, I was losing courage and any desire to talk about anything. If that were the case, my invitation would look pretty bad.

"Okay," she consented and lit up a cigarette, crossed her legs, and sat back. It was her favorite posture. I poured out some Martini and sat opposite her.

How many times I imagined a moment like this! How many times I revived a memory of the red light flashing before me in the end of that nocturnal alley! We were sitting almost as we were back then, but now a huge block wall rose between us. And Lika's name was dear to both of us.... Except for the fact that I knew about it, and she didn't. It pained me, and she composedly kept smoking and looking at me with her derisive squinting eyes – dark and deep, just like in the portraits of Flemish artists.

According to all prominent theories, among which there was also my study on manipulating systems, according to all the rules of man's reason and common sense, I was supposed to feel tired and indifferent. Theoretically, I could arrange all my thoughts in orderly pigeonholes: an eighteen-year-old greenhorn, not very experienced in amorous pleasures, in a time of hormonal activity meets his first love and.... the rest is clear, also taking into account the psychological constitution of the greenhorn himself. In general, it could be cured. If one really wanted to....

I looked at her, trying to find in her face something that would make me stop and think about all the awkwardness of my situation — and all I saw was the same mysterious and attractive woman. To make matters worse, I recalled the words Lika had said today: "Would you be able to live with just one leg?" I lived like that all those years. Liza was my missing body part, the loss of which induced phantom pain. And now when she was so close, I just couldn't let her go.

"Liza...," I said, "Liza, didn't you recognize me?"

8.

...Afterward, all I said didn't make any sense and was just stupid, I saw in front of me just her embarrassed wide-open eyes. I didn't let her come to her senses as I was afraid to hear even the sound of her voice. "I've loved you all my life," this was what all my discourse came to, "of all the people you've met in your life who can say the same thing?! I'm sure – no one! But this is madness... – Do you remember, that's the title you gave to your movie? – but this is the madness of my own free will! Because I couldn't, didn't want to forget you. I compared everyone to you, and even very admirable women paled and lost next to you. I felt like a scoundrel with them. And I've been punished. Even the meeting with you, about which I 'd dreamt all my life, ended up in an awful, despicable deed! But trust me, it's not my fault.... Liza, I'm still in love with you...."

Then I fell silent and the pause lasted forever. For so long, that in the course of these few minutes (or was it seconds?) I was born, grew up, and died.

"How disgusting...," she said at last, getting up from her seat. "How disgusting, disgusting.... What an obscene soap opera...."

There was a mortifying silence again.

"One word, right," she continued "I'll fix everything up with Lika myself – I'll pick her up from the airport when she comes back.... And .... and never come to our place again."

"Yes.... I understand...." I didn't recognize my voice, it was so hoarse. "Certainly. Yes. Of course."

She was already standing in the hallway and pulling nervously at the door-handle, trying to subdue the lock when I came out of my stupor and nearly blocked her path:

"You didn't get it! I didn't know that Lika was your daughter! I didn't know, I didn't ask. I followed her only because I saw the two of you together. And. And I love her, like everything that's related to you."

"Just look at this, what passions!" Her lips trembled as if she wanted to say something entirely different. Then she turned around so sharply that a couple of hairpins fell out of her hair, and her hair gently slapped my face (we were standing too close). "I don't even want to hear about love!" Liza's face was distorted, and it seemed she was going to burst into tears. "But it's – it's none of your business! That's it, I'm leaving!"

"Liza," I dared to utter her name once again, "I won't bother you anymore. Everything will be the way you want. But, I beg you, tell me: under *different circumstances*, knowing everything I just told you, would you be able to... if not love me, at least try to love me?... "

During a pause that hovered above us one could have died and be born anew. Her face suddenly softened, I recalled that glance – she looked at me just that way in THAT barn.

"What kind of fool are you? Is it possible that there still are people like you in this world? You know, I even envy you. And... I'm grateful to you. But I'm no longer twenty five... or however old I was then... So, there's nothing to talk about... Nonsense...."

"But still...," I needed to hear her answer badly, "after all, I'm losing you forever...."

"Maybe. Probably. I don't know...," she jerked the door open and darted out into the entryway. I ran after her. I wanted to see her out... But Liza flagged down the first car she saw and left.

I left to wander around town. I needed to cover a few kilometers, I wouldn't have been able to calm down otherwise.

...I came home in a delirium, went to the bedroom, and plopped onto the bed without taking off my shoes and jacket.

In the middle of the night it seemed like a huge black monster was coming at me. I hardly opened my eyes and saw a weird thing – in the corner of the room there was... a wardrobe. That very, "esteemed" one, with carved knobs. I concluded I was delirious, jumped out of bed and turned on the light. The phantom didn't vanish – it became more real. As if that wasn't enough! Where did it come from? When did it arrive? I couldn't wrack my already ailing brain over it. Maybe Lika had ordered it?... But – when did she have time to do that? And why this wardrobe now? And why – all this?...

Irene Rozdobudko

PART THREE
DENYS

1.

…I'm sitting in a small but extremely expensive cafe on the Arbat,[22] there is no one here but me. I'm trying to fall in love with Moscow, but it's not happening. I'm quoting Sorokin[23] to myself, he wrote that Moscow is a huge babe who's sprawled among the hills with her erogenous zones scattered wide so that it's nearly impossible to grope them. For this reason you can't fall in love with her at first sight, it's easier to grow to hate her. The maid Moscow is filthy, she reeks. It's the mark of a gourmand to admire this "musty smell."

I have three bruises over half my face – one on my cheekbone and two almost identical ones under my eyes, like pale blue "eyeglasses" that will soon turn dark blue (I know it through personal experience) and then will turn yellow. It'll take a while. A longer-than-one-week matter. In a word, my face in this condition wildly mismatches my suit and tie with a glass of Campari in front of me. Waitresses, who have, in fact, nothing better to do, are whispering something on this subject, having made themselves comfortable at the bar.

I haven't been here in about twenty or twenty five years. Everything is just as it was before, when folks of dubious appearance used to come this way in flocks every corner of

---

22 One of the most famous pedestrian streets in Moscow that dates from the 15th century.

23 Russian postmodernist writer Vladimir Sorokin (born 1955).

the most various countries, turning the city into a market-railway station, folks who had hoped to become a needle in a haystack. However, as my observations told me, the number of "needles" had long outnumbered the haystack. Having checked into the hotel in the morning, I went to see many dark places, railway-stations, and neighborhoods. It made no sense, but I couldn't just sit on my hands!

I earned this mosaic fresco on my face during my last "activity" – in the bunker of a radical party. I had gone there just because one of my friends had told me that supposedly hundreds of young vagabonds of various eminence and confessions, particularly a lot of various "creative individuals," and among them some representatives from our Institute of the Arts, lived there in a partial basement. It was there, while on assignment for his journalistic business, he saw a man, who supposedly took part in that artistic biennale five years ago. For several years that man wandered the open spaces of the universe and insisted that a few years ago he saw that red-haired countrywoman here. Before I got my face decorated with bruises, I managed to find out that the "red-haired girl" was from Latvia and was a complete drug-addict.

And now I had one hour left before a shoot of the TV program that I had never watched before and over which my mother had shed many tears — it was called "I'm Looking for You." As I was told, people watch it all from over the world. Before, I would have never dared to do such a weird thing. But I didn't think my students or colleagues might see me now. Let them see me! I don't give a damn. Just as I don't care that my face is covered with bruises. I pulled quite a few strings to get on the program, using all my personal connections. I waited for a few months on edge. And now I have to go to the broadcast studio. I finished my Campari, tossed some money on the table, and went to catch a cab.

At the entrance a manager and an assistant editor were already waiting for me – they had been informed about my visit.

"Denys Volodymyrovych?" The manager asked politely, thoroughly concealing his surprise with regard to my "war paint." "Nice to meet you, come in. We'll go now to the sixth floor to the dressing room, and then – to the third floor, to the studio. The show starts in half an hour."

There were a few make-up rooms on the sixth floor, but people were crowding near one room, waiting their turn to "powder their noses." There were mainly elderly women and women on the wrong side of thirty. They excitedly were relating their stunning stories. I felt quite creepy at the thought that I might end up in this sorrowful line. Thank God they took me to a different room – perhaps for "privileged" people.

"This is Olenka, our make-up artist," the editor introduced a nice young girl in a white gown to me, "she'll 'fix' you up a bit; after that then please come down to the studio. I'll show you to your seat."

To be honest, they both kept glancing at me with surprise and curiosity. And it also annoyed me.

I sat in the chair in front of a mirror and Olenka looked closely at my face.

"Where did you get that?..." she asked with compassion.

"I was walking, I slipped and fell. I came to my senses – in a plaster cast...," I answered.

The girl smiled, nodded and opened a huge box with makeup.

"You'll be as good as new in no time!"

Then she worked silently the whole time. I was grateful for that and even closed my eyes. After my morning street chase, my fight in the bunker and the glass of Campari, I felt quite woozy. I couldn't think of how I'd sit in front of the camera or what I'd say. I just wanted to get up and leave quietly. But I couldn't. I needed to close the chapter on it.

In a few minutes I couldn't recognize myself: the quite decent mug of a handsome man with a romantic bluishness under his eyes appeared in the mirror.

"How do you like it?" Olenka asked proudly while examining the end product of her work.

"Amazing! You're a magician!" I complimented her, rising from my chair.

"You need to go to the third floor," the girl reminded me, "good luck!"

I took the stairs, smoked two cigarettes in the hall, and went in the direction of the studio, which had already been buzzing like a beehive. In short time I was escorted to my seat – as had been arranged – in the first row, and they informed me when I was supposed to enter into the conversation. I looked around: almost all the women were holding handkerchiefs and photographs in their hands, it gave me cold shivers again. The production manager stepped out into the middle of the studio and gave the final instructions – at which signal to applaud, in which cameras to look, how to approach the tables, at which the hosts were sitting... .

"Attention! Camera!" She finally cried out in a voice different from her normal one, lifting up her wide-open hands, and started to bend down each fingers as she counted "Five, four, three, two... Action!"

The audience started to applaud frantically, and to this deafening noise, from behind a motley backdrop that was all pasted over with photographs, two hosts came out – an elderly man and a young actress who had previously managed to show up in a few TV series. They were speaking with feeling. The man sat at the table, the girl was running around the room with a microphone. Women lifted up photographs of their family and friends whom they wanted to find and begged them to come back. I waited for the microphone to appear under my nose with horror. And it finally happened.

"And who are you looking for?" The actress turned to me in a doctor-like tone, and the entire audience with all the cameras was now staring at me. I forced myself to get a photograph from my pocket... I had written what I was going to say in advance and memorized it. I didn't want to appear too sentimental, and so my voice sounded quite cold: name, last name, date of birth (year, month, day), date when she went missing. Toward the end – what others were saying, "If somebody has seen her or knows anything about her, please call me at...." When I was saying all this I felt like a stupid parrot.

The worst thing about it was that the general emotional mood of the audience seized me as well. Finishing my tirade, I felt my throat clench up and my voice began to quiver sinisterly and I, in the same manner as the rest, gasped into the microphone, "Lika, if you can hear me – come back!"

...I came back to the hotel late at night. It was cold in my room. I pulled a blanket over my head and piled pillows on top so that I couldn't hear any noises that could be heard from the hallway. I had a return-ticket for the morning train, so I tried to fall asleep. All that had happened that day seemed to me even more desperate than everything that had happened before. My participation in a popular TV-show placed the final period on my searching, a meaningless and tragicomic one....

2.

The most terrible thing in the first years was not to think – what happened to her. In order not to paint awful images in my imagination, I was actively involved in tracking her, and at the same time I was burying myself up to my ears in work during the day and in alcohol in the evenings. If that rhythm slowed down even for a minute – I was losing control over myself. In a moment like that I could easily crush a glass in my hand. And it happened once right in front of a baffled audience during an important meeting at the Film Institute Council on the matter of broadcasting. Any moment I could shove all those splinters into my mouth to ease yet a different, endless pain... It was particularly difficult to make it through the night. Then a real nightmare fell on me – the first year of searching and the dark dead-end of the second.

If SHE was no longer alive – how did it happen? Where? Who was by her side at that moment? Where is she now, my girl, who so didn't want to leave me? But if she is somewhere... It was no less painful to think about. I recalled thousands of instances of kidnapping, of selling people into slavery that could be found even in civilized Hamburg. If she's alive – what is she doing this very moment when I'm going insane on my sofa? How could it happen and why – to us, to her? I was going over every minute of our parting: how she packed her things, how I buttoned up her jacket, gave her the money, made sure that she got into a cab. The issue with the wardrobe remained unclear. I remembered clearly that I entered the bedroom only in the evening, totally wasted, and noticed it only at night. But where did this big log come from? Surely, cockroaches didn't bring it over there from the apartment next-door! In the store I found out that a girl had paid for it – it was probably Lika. But when did she bring it over and why did she do it? Is there any link between the purchase and her disappearance? I didn't see it. The damned wardrobe obscured my mind.

The fact that Lika was at the biennale during the first week was beyond doubt – I (the investigators, of course, also went down the same path) talked to everyone with whom she interacted there, and they confirmed it. She disappeared before the end of the art festival. As if into thin air! No one could say anything for sure. I found out that she went missing only ten to fifteen days after the rest of the participants returned. As Liza forbade me to show up anywhere near their home and said she'd meet Lika herself. I was convinced that Lika didn't want to ever see me again (though it seemed implausible to me), and the entire time I just kept thinking about what I should do. Finally I decided that everything was for the better and had the nerve to call the home of my former in-laws. I just wanted to hear the voice.... It's strange, but – the voice of Lika.

"Isn't she with you?!!" Liza yelled into the handset in an hysterical voice.

It turned out that Lika was not on the train that Lika had come to meet. There were many trains coming from that area, and Liza assumed that I had gone ahead and had met Lika before her....

Two weeks were lost because of that....

And then frightful searches started, to which, from time to time, they added awful questioning at the detective's office, interviews, and following everywhere with movie cameras. Lika's pictures hang in all the subway stations. My colleagues and students looked at me with sympathy, which was also unbearable, I was barely hanging in....

In the first months Liza kept calling me – I used to grab the handset with hope, but she called just to condemn me. Eventually, I stopped all communication with her family and from time to time heard rumors that Elyzaveta Tenetska hardly ever left her house and was slowly drinking herself to death along with her housemaid, a former actress who played a role in her first movie. In the meantime, her husband spared no effort in finding his daughter and was now combing through the Carpathian forests. But everything – was in vain.

Lika was gone....

Now I understand what the phrase "missing person" really means and I know how horrifying this expression is. "Missing" without a lead – it's a depressing dead-end. I came across something similar in Afghanistan, but then it didn't affect me personally. I remember it even seemed to me that there was some hope in it – to wait, to see, to hope for the better. But today I was of a different mind. If I had learned that Lika was no longer alive – it would have been that catharsis, after which I'd be able to breathe. Yet I was suffocating, imagining the worst. Lika was not adjusted to life at all, and she didn't even try to adjust, and that's why anything could have happened to her. But what could this "anything" comprise? – Anything – is everything. I found it easier to think that she had been abducted by aliens.

Her things haunted my mind for a long time. I kept constantly stumbling across them, and then exhausted myself, trying to remember when she wore this or that dress, dove into it with my face....

The next year I couldn't take it anymore, so I put everything, including her paints and paintings, out of sight in the wardrobe. In that very same one. Who would have thought then, when we were looking at it, sitting in a shop-window, that it would become a sarcophagus?

I didn't think about Liza anymore. It was strange and wild: as if Lika had taken away with her the obsession of my life. But did it need to happen at the cost of this?...

3.

...I'm on the plane. So far I don't know what new scents, sounds, sensations await me after we land. I don't know what kind of room I'll have at the hotel, what view it will have from the window. The sea? Palm thickets? Mountains? Or maybe a multicolored network of small restaurants on the seafront? I don't know. And I like these new sensations – staying in unfamiliar hotels, I like the moment when the room key from the administrator's hands finds its way into mine, I like taking the elevator up and follow the concierge along long halls, guessing where my temporary lodging is. What's it like? I love the moment of entering and the process of locking the door... That's all!

I like to flick all the switches at the same time, to open the doors of the bathroom and all the closets, inspecting "my" dominion. I like to open the doors to the balcony and see that it's clean and spacious with a glass coffee-table and with two cosy cane-chairs. I like the fact that my new dwelling and I are independent from each other, and that's why we keep a respectful relationship: my temporary lodging, just like a random companion, doesn't need the warmth of the heart and doesn't oblige you to anything. On the plane, at a height of 10,000 meters above sea level, it's cold, and in general, there's a disgusting dampness in my city – the summer this year is disappointing. I spent my vacation time without ever stirring from the house. And here it is this seminar by the Adriatic Sea – two boring weeks in a circle of colleagues from all over the world, speeches, the viewing of TV programs, music videos, commercials. It had been of no interest to me for a long time now. I just tried to maintain my profile. I even wanted to send a manager or one of my junior colleagues on business instead of going myself, but it was as if they had conspired against me – no one wanted to go. It's clear: they want me to unwind a bit. Fine, I'll try. If I can....

The seminar was supposed to take place in a small mountain town. As it turned out, it was approximately a one hour drive to the sea, but there was a huge lake inside the town – not completely clean, but picturesque, surrounded by blue-green mountains. The participants of the seminar were settled in an "old town," in a five-star hotel near the town hall, which looked just like the other medieval houses. In fact, it was an ancient fifteenth-century mansion, which matched all the requirements of the class of hotel.

I arrived there toward the evening. The way from the airport was dangerous – it wound in a narrow mountain "serpentine," fenced off with a low parapet here and there. A few times rusty car wrecks, lying in the crevices, caught my eye. Approaching the town, I mentioned the name of the hotel to the driver and, judging by his reaction, it was clear that it was a place for the rich. There was no driveway to the "old town" – all the cars stopped at the square by a tall stone gate. As soon as I put my feet on the paving stone of this historic place, a trained attendant in a uniform ran up to me (only God knows how he recognized me), he picked up my suitcase and escorted me into the town, which, from all sides, was surrounded by high walls. That's the place to shoot movies! On our way he explained in fine English what landmarks we were passing by and where the best restaurants, which were in abundance on the narrow streets, were located. In some strange way restaurants, cafes and pubs fit in these streets, whose width didn't exceed the span of your arms, and had a cosy and romantic façade. We found ourselves at the hotel in about three minutes, during which time I turned my head in every direction, trying to remember the location of various venues. My hotel room turned out to be luxurious – with ancient oak furniture, silver thread embroidered blankets, and a big ancient chandelier. I gave the concierge a tip and closed the door with relief. I opened the door to the balcony – it faced the square in front of the town hall. Three restaurants lined up in a circle at the square. There were tables outside with people sitting at them. Appetizing scents – delicate and unobtrusive — were wafting over the entire town. I quickly unpacked, changed, and decided to ramble through the streets and to have dinner at one of the restaurants.

It was impossible to get lost there – all the streets spiralled round the town hall. I walked for a long time, admiring the ancient nature and cosiness of this town, which more and more reminded me of some kind of historic labyrinth. Lika would probably like this place, it occurred to me suddenly. No, that's not true – this "suddenly" became my permanent, usual state. Now when I've come across any signs of life, I found myself thinking that I measure them in terms of: what would Lika say?...

4.

...The thing that always surprised me was that even ironically-disposed respectable citizens perceive TV men as some kind of deities, they were dying to be on TV, and the next day after they appear on a talk show, they look around proudly: will strangers recognize them? I knew that world quite well, and I knew that in due time everything slowly turns into profanation. One thing was important for me: to admit it unreservedly. I, for example, could expressly declare: everything I've been doing all these years is profanation, quite talented at that (you can't deny it), but it still is profanation. I masterfully agitated humanity to buy detergents, anti-cavity chewing-gums, yoghurt, tires, etc. I had to oversell all those products to as many people as possible – whether I could afford buying all of that depended on it. That's more or less what I thought when I was planning to participate in this seminar and, of course, I didn't plan to speak about it out loud. Except ,perhaps, over a shot of *rakia*[24] with people like me. If I, of course, could find people like me. I know Lika would understand me. I started to figure things out for myself: against the background of all this profanation, I finally found that *something* that I had always been looking for – a woman who loved me just the way I was, with all the baggage I had within. She loved me – all the same. Not a hero, or a wise or a rich man. She loved me. And without giving me some time to realize it, she suddenly disappeared from my life. Suddenly, horribly, and quietly. As quietly as she loved. She lived in me like a grain of sand inside a shell – causing pain to my tender egoistic innards, and now she's rolled out to the outside. Now I think about the way she would want it. Do you know about this, Lika?... Hey!...

...Having sat through the formal opening session of the seminar, I decided there was nothing for me to do there. The more so as no one really needed me to be there. My badge enabled me to attend all the museums. I decided to use this opportunity instead of going by minibus to the place where the seminar was held every morning. So, it looked approximately like this: every morning at eight, a van came to the hotel, two hip girls in scanty jean shorts that exposed their tanned bottoms halfway, and a couple of Italian cameramen were already in there. On our way

---

24 An alcoholic beverage made from fruit and popular in the Balkans.

we stopped by at a few more hotels to pick up a few more colleagues and with such a "fast crowd" we went to Cetin (or – Cetinje, as locals pronounced it). There, in a conference hall of one of the five-star hotel-monsters, there were about one hundred of us, and we were marinated till evening there with a lunch break and a fifteen minute coffee break every hour. After two or three talks and the viewing of commercials, I sneaked out to escape downtown. And after the first try, I did it every day.

Montenegro (for some reason I like this particular name for this country) – a small country that not so long ago was part of the former Yugoslavia. Despite the fact that the city of Podgorica was considered the official capital of Montenegro, Cetinje was its heart. This picturesque town wasn't much different from the rest – a few streets, an abundance of cafes, yellow slabs of squares, plenty of walnut trees, and remarkable gothic buildings.

I wandered out, stopping at cafes to have a glass of the local light beer, which was to my liking. Once I came across a monastery where the hand of John the Baptist is preserved. I stared blankly at this dark brown dried up limb, and yet again I thought: what would Lika say? I imagine she wouldn't like this spectacle....

I hitchhiked back to the town where my hotel was. And the locals didn't take a penny from me.

One week went by this way, and by the end of it, this calm, almost vegetative, life lulled me with its slow and lengthy evenings permeated by the aroma of coffee. Swarthy moustachioed natives sat all day long in these "kafanas" (that's what they called the cafes there) over a glass of *rakia*, resembling stone statues – just as still and ancient as the mountains.

In general, I had the impression that it was as though I made my way into a snuffbox of a Turkish Pasha – so slow was the life in that town. Any movement seemed surprising, and strange music resembled that of the Orient. Once I watched a "Montenegrin choir" from my balcony:

four men formed a tight circle, holding each other by the arm, four other men clambered onto their shoulders, and another four got on top of the "third floor." This entire human edifice started to sway to the music that could be heard from the restaurant. A breath of something authentic, ancient and eternal came from this dance. I imagined that I was putting my hand onto Lika's shoulder in an uncontrived and usual motion, and we were watching all this together. Her eyes are wide-open like a child's. She's smiling and squeezing my hand....

5.

...Tsyn-tsy-lin-tsy!

Precious klintsy!

My main occupatsia –

Is a fast tsyntsyliatsia!

"Klintsy" means drumsticks, "tsyntsyliatsia" is something like to drum. I was in a *kafana*, listening to this simple ditty. I've walked this town for miles around, and I had three more days before I was supposed to leave. I didn't know what to do during that time. I finished my beer, left the "old town" and walked down to the lake. At the lakefront, representatives of private tourist companies were sitting under straw sheds like spiders in their cobweb. They didn't impose their service on you the way it is in Tunis or Egypt. A great number of photographs were glued on the advertising stands behind them, each had an inscription underneath: "Diving," "Surfing," "Boat Tour," "Monasteries" – along with the cost of the service. I had never taken time to have a good look at those stands before. But for some reason, the thought of scuba-diving as the last thing to do before leaving crossed my mind. I approached the owner of a stand and sat down in a wicker chair in front of him.

"What is sir interested in?"

I explained that the sir was interested in taking solo diving, not with a group.

"Would you, sir, be willing to take a private scuba diving tour?"

Yes, that was exactly what sir wanted.

"No problem!" The owner exclaimed and began to explain what my tour to the sea would be like, what the cost was, and to which bay they could take me right away, if I'd like that.

"Oh, it's a very beautiful place! Just look...."

He opened an album in front of me with different photos portraying happy tourists (mostly women), who were posing in water surrounded by fish. I lazily flipped through it, turning involuntary again and again to one photo: a woman with long blond hair that heaved above her head like a canvas, her eyes looked too seriously through the glass of the goggles straight into the camera, the snorkel she gripped between her lips distorted the lower part of her face, near her outstretched hand – was a small yellow fish....

"Is sir purchasing the tour?" The owner's voice shook me out of some kind of stupor (that happened to me quite often).

"What? Yes... I have to think about it...."

I got up and went along the lakefront.

I came to the corner. Lit up a cigarette. Leaned against the fence and looked around. Every second or at least every fifth girl even in this small foreign town looked like Lika. Every time I encountered this resemblance I rejoiced in my mind's eye – it seemed to me that Lika was alive for sure – she's breathing, walking, laughing, just like these carefree strangers....

I came back to the owner of the diving tent at a brisk pace.

"May I take another look at the photos?"

"Sure!" He handed me a few albums. I unmistakably got hold of the one that had a picture of a blond girl who had captured my attention. I immediately opened it on that photo and couldn't take my eyes off it. She looked so much like Lika! Only the color of her hair threw me off. As well as a certain athletic aspect of her physique. I wanted to thank him and return the album, but I couldn't take my eyes off the gaze behind the glass of the goggles. "Nonsense..." I thought "it's not possible...."

"Could you tell me please, what are these pictures? Where did you get them from?" I asked.

"These photos are actual ones – from the place where my clients dive! Don't hesitate! It's beautiful over there. You won't regret it...."

"It's not what I meant. I wanted to know who took these pictures."

The owner cast a bewildered glance at me.

"Vlaiko took this one, he's my cameraman. Is sir not happy with something? Is there something I can do to help?"

"Yes," I said quickly, "sell me this picture."

I wanted to take it as soon as I could and examine it closely in private.

"You can have it!" The man smiled, "did sir like the lady?"

"I don't know yet... She just looks like... a woman I'm trying to find."

I took the picture and put coin Euro on the table.

"Thank you," the owner nodded to me, "good luck!"

I left and came back again: "Do you think the cameraman might know who this woman is, where she's from and what her name is?"

"No way, sir! We don't ask unnecessary questions. Though...," he paused to think, "Vlaiko is a chatty boy. But the picture was taken a year ago. I doubt he'll recall anything...."

"Where can I find this Vlaiko?" I asked, putting another coin on the table.

"Ehhh... He's been not one to be trifled with lately." The owner shook his head. "He hasn't been working with me since an accident at sea. He lives in Budva. I'll write down his address...."

On my way to the hotel I dropped in at an antique shop and bought a loupe.

It was cool and quiet in my room, I pulled the heavy blinds together, turned on a wall lamp, got the picture and the loupe out of my pocket. The scuba-diver's face came closer to me so that I could see what color her eyes were. They were greenish, like those of the frog princess....

6.

I had two more days... I was not certain about anything. But if I were a psychic, I could swear that warmth emanated from the picture on which I kept a fast hold. Common sense told me that it was not her, that it couldn't happen, because... But, why not?...

In the morning I set off for Budva – a small resort town on the seafront. I arrived there around noon, when the sun already was beating down mercilessly, and the beaches were crowded with people. I took a cab and gave the driver the address. I spoke English to him, since it was the language that even shop assistants understood well. The driver drove me somewhere to the outskirts where there were no hotels, and ragged dark blue patches of the sea showed from in-between newly built quarters. The building where the cameraman lived turned out to be quite a decent high-rise building, though it was damp and dark inside, and inscriptions and images were spray painted on the walls. Almost everything was just like back home... I went up to the fourth floor and pressed the button of the doorbell. No one answered the door for a long time, and then I heard some kind of a wooden sound and a rustle as if somebody were walking slowly with a limp. The man who opened the door was indeed leaning on his crutches.

"Are you Vlaiko?" I asked.

"Yes," he answered, "why?"

I pulled the picture from my pocket.

"Did you take this picture?"

He casually rested his arm on the door, took the picture, and brought it closer to his eyes.

"Maybe... But I'm no longer in business. What's this all about?"

"May I come in?" I asked. The man shrugged his shoulders, moved a little and hopped back inside the apartment on his crutches. I followed him. We stepped into the kitchen.

Vlaiko carefully dropped in a chair, put the crutches aside and pointed at the chair in front of him.

"What happened to you?" I decided to ask.

"That... I got under a propeller. Up till now they haven't been able to cure me. I've had surgery three times already. So, what did you want to talk about?"

"The owner of the diving tent kiosk told me that this picture had been taken by you." I began to explain, a bit concerned whether he understood my English well. "I was hoping you might remember who that woman was, where she was from, and what her name was... I understand that it may seem a bit strange, but...."

"It is strange, for sure!" Vlaiko frowned. "How can I remember all those whose picture I took? Do you know how many people I had every day! And every month?! And every season?!! There's no way I could know all their names! What a thing to say...."

"Yes, sure, I understand...."

Obviously, I looked frustrated.

"Just a moment...," Vlaiko took pity on me and once again reached out his hand for the picture, "Let me take another look...."

He looked at the picture with a shade of doubt.

"I've got thousands of pictures of babes like this one..." He mumbled. "This one is as pretty as the rest... I can't recall even those with whom I had... What's the point in remembering it? White bathing suit... blond hair... yellow fish... trashy composition... But the quality is good. I won't have a job like that, that's for sure... No, I don't remember!" He finally gave the picture back to me. "I can't help you. Just think, how can I remember stuff like that? Why do you need this girl?"

"She looks very much like my wife...."

"Ehhh... All the more I won't tell you a thing. Do you know how many of them come here with other men?! Why don't you ask her who she was here with?.. I don't play those games. I don't give a damn."

I got up. Of course! What could I expect....

"Sorry to have bothered you."

A quiver appeared in my voice, and Vlaiko decided to cheer me up:

"Don't you worry. My condition is much worse than yours. Sometimes it gets so bad that I just want to howl. You'll find somebody. This one wouldn't be good for you anyway, I think, she's an American...."

"So," I pricked up my ears, "you do remember something after all?!"

"As my grandfather Milan used to say – may he rest in peace! – two shots of vodka and I'll remember the eye color of Adam's daughter."

What a fool am I! Why didn't I figure it out right away?! I stormed out of the apartment and darted to the nearest supermarket, came back with a bottle of *rakia* and vacuum-packed sheep milk cheese. Vlaiko noticeably brightened up. After the third shot we drank "to love," I poked his nose into the picture as if he were a German shepherd search dog. This time, sensing all the responsibility of the moment, he ran his palm over it.

"American she is," he finally uttered after these magic movements. "Yes. An American, for sure."

"I've heard this already. What else?"

"Why do you care so much, pal?" He was getting mellow. "We are Slavs! And where is America? Far off! She was American – I'll bet my life on it! Blonde, cute... She didn't look like an American, but she was American... Wait a second!" He recollected suddenly, "I think I'm starting to remember... It was around a year ago. I got hit then. We were guiding a group from the Santa-Rio – it's a hotel on the seafront... There it was that I got hit, this lady was holding my hand in an ambulance all the way to the hospital! It was then when I thought that her eyes were like an angel's and that her hands were soft and tiny... While she was holding her palm on my forehead – I felt like I was not in pain..." He closed his eyes and then looked at the picture once again. "That's it! What an ungrateful wretch I am! I couldn't care less about her at that time, but I remember that she got into the ambulance with me, made sure that I was taken to the best hospital, and on top of that, she gave me some money to cover medical care! Later I thought: why would she do that for me...."

"And you are not lying?" I asked with suspicion. Because he remembered everything very quickly.

"I'm not lying!" The cameraman was insulted. "I have a professional memory, have no doubts! And why I didn't remember earlier – there are many of you, jealous men, around here... And even more private investigators, they're chasing down cheating husbands and wives all the time...."

"Do you remember her name?"

"No. But you can find it out in the hotel. They have registration books there...."

That's right! I couldn't keep still in the handicapped cameraman's apartment, I left him a few pieces of money and thanked him. I shook his hand and jumped out into the street in no time. As if I had stepped on a burning hot frying pan....

7.

The Santa-Rio Grand Hotel was located on the seafront. The sea was glistening just a short distance away, today it was densely packed with swimmers – boisterous and carefree – the ceaseless clamor and roar of Jet Ski engines were in the air. A slow rustle of waves was buried under a layer of this human cacophony. I entered a hall and found myself in a refreshing silence, in which a stream of a built-in fountain was melodiously murmuring. I approached the administrator. A peculiar looking man with a moustache, twisted in a few rings at each end, looked amiably at my badge. I pulled out the picture.

"Could you help me? I'm looking for this woman. She was here a year or more than a year ago...," I said without any introduction.

An expression of surprise appeared on his face. I shoved the picture under his nose. He politely took it in his hands, but first he glanced at me in a carping way:

"We may have a few thousand guests in one season...."

"I'm relying on your professional memory," I decided to flatter him, and that was the right call. The administrator started to examine the picture closely, his moustache twitched amusingly.

"Maybe...." He mumbled, "maybe...."

I waited. I couldn't rush him. My heart was knocking like a sledgehammer.

"Of course!" The clerk's face shone at last, "good God, that's our favorite Angie McLain! She was here with her husband last year, and everyone was enchanted by her!"

The strange foreign name sobered me up. I stood there as if I were made of stone, realizing that it was a stupid thing to do, turning into a complete idiot who had completely lost control over himself.

"That is how... Turns out, I was mistaken... Sorry."

"Mrs. Angie is an artist," the administrator continued with delight, "Just take a look at the painting she gave as a gift to the hotel!" He waved his hand somewhere toward the center of the hall.

I turned around. My heart made such a strong jolt, that I barely remained on my feet. No way! Such familiar brush work, so loved by me, the clarity and precision of all the lines, pure colors... I could barely come to my senses.

"Do you know anything about her?"

"If you're interested in this artist, you should talk to Zdenka. She's a maid. She worked on the third floor at that time... And I would add from myself – she's a real angel. You don't meet people like her very often. Always smiling, she would always ask you if something was wrong, would always help... She learned our language in just a few days. Many people here remember her."

"So, she's American, right?"

"Her husband is definitely from there. But she... I'm not sure. I've seen American girls before, they're different. Go talk to Zdenka, she's on duty on the third floor..., "

"I have one more question: you probably register your guests and write down their addresses?"

"Of course. If you would like to have her address, I can try to find her business card. I think she left it." And the administrator started to rummage in a drawer slowly. I watched him as if he were a fakir in a circus. It seemed that, one more moment, and he'd pull out something very familiar from there – a ribbon, a hairpin, a note... But he handed me a small card, with an unfamiliar name and email address in English printed on it.

I thanked him and went up to the third floor and found the maids' room. A round-faced brunette wearing a lace apron was in fact there. Hardly had I explained what I wanted from her, when Zdenka, having opened her eyes wide, started singing the praises of this very Angie McLain and, of course, recognized her in the picture right away.

"I have one just like that!" She said proudly. "Angie gave it to me herself. I asked – and she gave it to me.

Normally, we're not allowed to talk to the guests, but Angie, she is so... You can't imagine!! My son Tseka – a scamp, if ever there was one, I'm telling you! – he back then enrolled in a music class. He's crazy about music, but we didn't have a violin back then. They're expensive – I can't afford it. I unintentionally (sir, don't think I ever asked for it!) mentioned it, so Mrs. McLain went to the store with him and picked out the best violin! It made me cry so much then... As I've been bringing up Tseka, this hooligan, from the cradle, I've run my feet off already! I thought he was a lost soul! And she – she gave him the violin! And you know what, sir? He is now the best student in class! Recently they've given a concert in Podgorica itself!" Zdenka's eyes filled with tears, she got a handkerchief, wiped them off, and continued:

"Every time I hear him playing, it's as if I hear Mrs. McLain's voice. It's for a reason that she has such a name – Angie, that is, an angel...."

I had a coughing fit. Zdenka tapped me on my back.

"Is there anything else that sir would want to know? Does sir know Angie? If you do, please tell her that Zdenka prays to God for her...."

"No," I said in a hoarse voice, "I don't know Angie...."

I said goodbye. In the hall I nodded to the amiable administrator, cast a final glance at the painting... And hurriedly went to the highway.

My flight was next morning. I had to go back to my hotel to pack my things. All the way I held the business card in my hand, lifting it close to my eyes from time to time, reading the strange name, the strange address, written in a strange language. Angie McLain. What nonsense! Angie – "angel." Maybe it is – Anzhelika? But she didn't like that name very much....

8.

...I brushed away all my sentimental theories with – "it can't be true!" I was busy with other things now. I had to collect my thoughts and to find everything out. And yet... And yet... it can't be true!

The next day, at five in the evening, I opened the door to my apartment. I didn't feel like eating. Strangely enough, I didn't feel like drinking either. It was a good thing that I found a can of coffee at home. I put the picture and the business card on the table. I stared at it like a stuck pig yet again. What could have happened? Why? After all, I knew Lika very well – she couldn't just leave. Let alone with a man. It all seemed to be from the realm of the imaginary.

Then my thoughts started to work in a different direction, which made it even worse. It was odd: total strangers remembered her, spoke of her as if she were mother Theresa... Why didn't I notice it? Of course, her frankness and naiveté touched me deeply. But more often than not – they irritated me. Now I just wanted to groan. Maybe she was in fact unique, she chose me for her quiet and devoted love. I could have been happy and tranquil now! I peered into the picture and saw one more thing: the woman on it was incredibly attractive. Not a baby, not a frog princess... I was recalling every moment with her and realized that Lika – was now unreachable and inapprehensible – that, which I had been looking for all my life.

But what happened? What happened on that last day? In the morning I literally showed her the door. I was happy that she was leaving... But she so didn't want to leave! What happened after I buttoned up her jacket and closed the door after her?

That terrible conversation with her mother, that frightful night after my exhausting barhopping for hours. What is it? Of course. This damned wardrobe that scared me at night. During the search I had no time or desire to think about it. No doubt that it was Lika who ordered it. But who delivered it? When? Maybe she did it? That is, she came back home? If so, why didn't she even leave me a note if she wanted to surprise me this way?!

"Did I even look for it?!" I nearly cried out.

I rushed to the room. It was fairly late, the "esteemed wardrobe" loomed in the dark like the Titanic that devoured her things, which I didn't dare look through. I started taking them out convulsively, thoroughly shaking each one of them. These searches resulted in nothing except in pain and frenzied palpitations. When all the contents of the wardrobe had been thrown on the floor, I once again looked closely at the massive bottom and deep in the corner I saw... a button. The very button from her jacket. *"This angel adores you...."*

I squeezed it in my hand. A cry that escaped my throat could have turned the earth upside down....

9.

...I wrote a short message to the email address indicated on the business card. And then every hour of my life turned into painful anticipation.

And now a little yellow folder lit up in the right corner. I didn't know what was better – this folder or NOTHING. I took a breath. I clicked with the mouse. I closed my eyes. I opened them up....

"I died on the 25th of September 1997...."

I buried my face in my hands. The cold and darkness devoured me....

BOOK TWO
LIKA

"I died on the 25th of September 1997...

Every time I remember that day, I cover my face with my hands – even when I'm around people....

...All the way to the railway station, the feeling that I had been launched into space didn't leave me. A red light was blinking on the control unit in the cab, I don't know what it was – the light of the meter or the stereo – it seemed to me that flickering was counting off minutes of my stay on Earth. I was subconsciously looking for a chance to stay. But I had the ticket in my pocket, my paints and French easel had been delivered to the location before me, the weather was wonderful, and the cab was driving fast.

I had one more hour before the train, so I roamed around the railway station square. I saw something that could change my plans: "our" wardrobe in the glass shop-window, there was a sign on it: "For Sale!" I felt incredible relief: an excuse was found! I had some money, so I finalized the purchase right away. And then a "brilliant idea" crossed my mind: I'll be at home, and then, before your arrival, I'll hide in the wardrobe. That was the surprise I was planning....

After that? I died....

I went back to the railway station, bought another ticket and got on the train...."

1.

...She was nicknamed Fox at the university. Because of her hair and green eyes.

Fox appeared in the evening of the day following the opening of the biennale. At that time young artists and guests were having dinner, gathering around a large charcoal grill and buffet tables set out in a meadow. A short distance away, a chamber orchestra was playing

Vivaldi melodies. Around forty meters from an improvised living room, there were massive canvas pavilions with expositions, and a bit further away – tents for the participants. Foreign guests and journalists stayed in the picturesque hotel complex of the regional center. Buses waited for them behind hillsides. Visitors had a fairly presentable appearance in comparison with the art folk. At dusk, the white shirts of the men glowed as if they were neon. Gentle music, the clatter of wine glasses, subdued voices, and a shaggy black mountain... It breathed as if it were alive and resembled a giant beast that had fallen asleep in the country of Lilliput. As soon as the esteemed public along with the orchestra had left – the scenery changed. About thirty people stayed in the meadow. Entirely different sounds were now coming from a tape-recorder; in addition to the leftover champagne, bottles of vodka appeared on the tables, the odor of smoked weed was in the air, and the artists grouped near the bonfire. At that moment, she appeared in the meadow.

"Look, there's Fox!" Bird noticed her first – a lean boy called Sashko "in the real world." "She's come after all...."

"As always, in her usual vein...," Vika, a ceramist, joined in the conversation, "as if she had fallen off the moon...."

"Shut up, Fox will always be Fox, even in the tundra!" Vlad, another acquaintance of theirs, added. Throwing a cigarette butt into the bushes, he got up to meet the girl who was looking about perplexedly. "I'll go meet our queen, or else she'll get lost...."

Fox was pale, her jeans covered with dirt up to her knees, her pointy face froze into a mask of indifference. She was seated at the bonfire, somebody handed a glass of vodka and a shish kebab on a wooden stick to her. Fox drank it up silently, which made Vika give a whistle, and the whole company burst into laughter.

"Good girl!" Bird said. "One of our own. Why do you always act like a stranger...."

"And when did she become family to you, if I may?" Vika laughed insidiously. "Fox is a bird of a different feather. With such a daddy. And her husband is of the same kind. So, you have nothing to worry about, Bird."

"Would you like a joint?" Bird continued, ignoring what his friend was saying.

"She's silent – well, that means consent!" Vlad concluded, offering another cigarette to the newcomer. The guys exchanged looks. Then came a pause during which Fox obediently took a few puffs.

"There's our little angel!" Vika laughed. "She must be fed up with her married life!"

Everyone began to laugh merrily. Bird topped off the glass that Fox was holding in her hand with vodka:

"Drink, sweetie, you won't get that at home!"

Surrendering to the company, Fox took a few sips, and Vika shoved a grape into her mouth. Vlad sat next to her and put his arm around her shoulders:

"There you go, here comes a blush! Why sit here like you were embalmed. You've become estranged from people. Don't worry, we'll turn you into a human being in a few days!"

"Her getup needs to be changed." Vika observed critically, "and her mug is like a school girl's. Listen, want me to do dreadlocks for you?!"

"That's it!" Bird exulted, "Vikusia is our dreadlocks master! Come on, Fox, say yes! You'll knock your father senseless!"

"Sure!" Vika got up from the grass and dragged the girl by the hand. "Let's go to the tent! Dreads are cool! You'll be second to none in the plein air tomorrow! Let's do it!"

Fox offered no resistance. It was strange, unusual, and it excited her compatriots. The happy crowd headed to the tent. The object of the experiment was seated on a stool, and they sat themselves on folding-beds, sipping beer from cans. Vika set to work. At first she tightly backcombed locks of hair with an iron comb until they turned into knotty tangles. The process was fairly unpleasant and painful, but Fox sat quietly and submissively, with just her head twitching in all directions like a doll. Vika took a crochet needle out of her backpack (she always carried along thread and crocheted lace hats that she sold) and neatly pulled stray hairs into the dreads. In the meantime, Vlad melted a wax candle in a can. And Vika rubbed this slop in every dreadlock with fast and skilful movements. Fox sat with her eyes closed as if she were sleepy. Vika used a lighter to burn extra hairs and once again tightened the locks with the crocheting needle.

When the work was done, the reddish dawn was rising outside the window of the tent, and the tired spectators snored despairingly on their folding-beds.

2.

At nine in the morning, the tent camp was finally awake. The sleepy artists crawled to the spot set up as a dining area, lining up to the beer stand. In an hour they all had to leave for the plein air session in the mountains. The artists looked as if they had slept in the clothes they were wearing. The girl who arrived yesterday noticeably stood out from the crowd. She was beyond recognition! Ethnic braids-dreads stuck out in every direction around her face. On seeing her, everyone applauded. One person handed her a can of beer, another took the heavy French easel off her shoulder. Having had some eggs and strong coffee, the happy crowd of artists streamed to the mountains. And there they disbanded just as chaotically in search of the best vantage point on the landscape.

"Listen," Vlad whispered to Vika who was setting up her French easel on the grass, "did you notice, Fox hasn't uttered a word... Or does it just seem like that to me?"

"Don't worry," Vika flicked her hand at him, "she never talks a lot...."

They both looked in the direction of Fox who was some twenty meters away from them.

"How about that!" Vlad uttered thoughtfully. "They won't recognize her like that at home. You made quite a beast out of her...."

"I think it looks pretty good! And – no need to wash hair. By the way, a hairdo like that costs more than three hundred *hryvnias* at a hair salon! And here – it's for free...."

"Still, I think something's not right with her...."

"You just keep working, psychologist!" Vika cheered him up, "and let others work! The foreigners will scuttle in here in a few hours – we have to finish. What if they decide to buy something?!"

...An autumn morning in the mountains – a thick jelly, a cool and clear mass, that, it seemed, you could hold in your hand, so delicious was the air, so gorgeous was the landscape, as if it were woven from massive wool yarn. And if you wanted to step a bit aside from that place where Fox was mechanically setting up her French easel and push off from the end of the stony earth – you could fly up. You could fly long – three minutes or so – down to the cobalt blue ribbon of the river, embroidered with tiny golden rays. It hurts your eyes to look at those dazzling flashes. It seemed that the river was embroidered among the sylvan tracts similarly with thicker threads. Fox put the brush aside and took a palette knife: you have to mold this kind of landscape with pure paint! Back in the day she would never have dared to do such a thing. But now she was molding something phantasmagorical on the canvas. Before noon it became clear that it would be her only painting, otherwise she would have to go to town to buy some more paint. On hearing the gong that invited the artists for lunch, Fox wiped her hands on her jeans, and Vika glanced expressively at Vlad, twirling her index finger near the crown of her head.

Groups of guests from yesterday were roaming about the hills. They came up to the French easels, hanging over the backs of the painters, discussing what they had seen. Some gave interviews.

"Marvellous!" Fox heard a man's voice over her shoulders. Actually, the word sounded a bit differently, with a barely noticeable accent, "do you plan to sell it?"

"Hey, Fox! Someone is addressing you!" Vika called out to her friend, having noticed that she was ignoring the remark of the handsome man who had approached her. The girl turned around slowly. A wide "name brand" smile appeared from his smiling face. He froze for about three minutes.

"Sorry…," he finally uttered, taking a few steps back, "sorry…."

He remained behind her back for another few seconds. Then he decisively took a white plastic card out of his wallet:

"Sorry to bother you… I'd be happy to look at your other works. I want to buy them. Here's my business card. Please take it. I'll be in your country a year or a year and a half and will be able to come to your studio anytime. Here's my contact information, my cell phone…."

Fox mechanically put the card into her pocket.

3.

"A few days before the end of biennale, at night, I slipped out of the tent. I slept all the time without changing my clothes, I had nothing with me. I had to escape as soon as possible – away from these tents, from the scent of paints and alcohol, from incomprehensible words, and actions of people I didn't know.

I headed toward the mountain. And the further I went away from the camp, the clearer it was to me – that's exactly what I needed. I happened to be where I was supposed to be. I discerned the scents like an animal and was able to see in the total darkness. It seems to me, I was even running on all fours, running all night long, until the scent of the camp town stopped tormenting me. I sank my hands into the earth on steep hills and felt that it was alive and floating. I walked until pink ribbons of the morning began to flutter over the tops of fir-trees. They expanded, unfolded, and fell over the mountains and forest in wide veils. I wanted to drink, so I bent over a spring, I saw an entire small underwater town at the bottom – eggs laid by dragonflies, and also leeches and snails.... Then I piled leaves onto myself and slept till the next morning. And at night I sallied forth again.

If somebody asked me now where I was headed – I wouldn't be able to answer. I was going up the hill, coming down to the valley, and going up again. I wasn't as scared here as down there where I didn't understand anything....

4.

Autumn hung in the dark blue expanse like a light cambric shawl. From time to time a light wind lifted it up, and a different picture opened up for a moment amid the vivid nature: it was paler that the one before, with silver hoarfrost that was slowly covering the mountains. I don't know how long I walked and how I found myself near a small village scattered like a deck of cards. From on top of the hill I saw huts, some of them empty like a blind man's pupils, a store with a sign *Silpo*, a well in the middle of a road....

The huts were wide apart and not fenced. I came quite close to the last one that was located higher than the rest, leaned against some building (it was probably a barn or a chicken coop) and slid down. I felt the warmth of a tree with my back, the sun was washing my face, as if I had dipped it in warm water. I didn't feel my legs. Everything vibrated inside me as if I had been walking a tightrope all this time.

It was an odd sensation, not quite human, but it brought relief. I perceived human language as an unorganized stream of sounds, but every movement of nature, like the murmur of a stream, the rustle of leaves, the chirping of birds, the mysterious roar of the forest and mountains – all was intelligible to me. I followed just my instincts and everything was so easy. Sleep, eat, walk, sit, soak up rays of sun, walk again.... All this replaced my thoughts as my thoughts could have killed me. I dozed off near the warm wall, but in a sensual, animal-like way. My ear turned into a detector that was discerning the remotest sounds. It seemed like I heard a bee buzzing somewhere far away....

I heard a bed squeak inside the house, planks creak, feet shuffle on the wooden floor. In a few minutes an old woman bent over me dressed in a long dark blue skirt with many little flowers on it, from under her thick brown shawl another one appeared – white and thin, tucked-in tenderly at her temples. The grandmother stood with her arms crossed over her belly, looking at me with surprise.

"Who are you?" She finally asked. "I can't make out, you a boy or a girl?" It was tiresome to answer her, fatigue shackled my tongue. Words had no meaning to me.

"Where have you been walking?" The old woman asked again, examining my dirty clothes, "do you want to eat?"

She pulled a white egg out of her pocket and handed it to me. It was still warm. I grabbed it, squeezed it in my palms, and sucked the liquid greedily out of the eggshell. Had it fallen on the ground, I could have licked it off the way cats and dogs do....

"Oh Lord!" The grandmother flung her arms up, staring at me sympathetically, "Where are you going? Do you have a home? Why are you looking like that? No home? An orphan? What am I to do with you?... There, your clothes are completely torn.... Leaves in your hair.... What am I to do with you?"

I just looked at her. After the egg, the taste of which I didn't even discern, I got really hungry. You have to earn the food. I noticed an empty bucket in the yard. Buckets are used to carry water, that I remembered. The well was a few meters away from the house. I got up, took the bucket and pointed my finger at the well and then back at the bucket, so that the grandmother wouldn't think I wanted to steal it.

I had never gotten water out of a well before, but I did everything right: I attached it to the hook, lowered it down the well, and then for a long time – for ages – turned a handle until the bucket showed up on the surface. I couldn't help it and clung to the water and drank so much that I had to lower the bucket down the well once again.

I hardly dragged the bucket up to the house and placed it at the threshold. The grandmother sat next to it and started to quickly husk corn. A big cauldron with beets was sitting close by. A knife stuck out of one beet, like out of a dead body.

"Thank you, child," she said and nodded toward the cauldron, "the beets need to be chopped up for the pigs. I have no time to do it all myself.... But can I trust you with a knife? Who knows...."

I pulled the knife out, sat next to her and started to chop up the beets.

5.

...That's how I stayed in this lost-among-the-mountains and half-dead village. The grandmother lived alone, her children had moved out long time ago, and her husband had died a few years ago.

"If you have nowhere to go," she said, "stay with me. You'll help me around the house. It's hard to do it all myself. I'll feed you. You can sleep on the veranda. And then we'll see...."

In the evening when I was cutting off dry cornstalks, the grandmother gave me a plate with goat cheese on it and a glass of milk.

"Now, let's go indoors. I'll show you your spot."

She took me inside.

"You can lie down here," she pointed to a low trestle bed in the corner of the roomy glass veranda, "a blanket and a pillow are here. Tomorrow I'll take you to the bathhouse if you want."

Truth be told, the bathhouse works once a month here, but Yakivna, the manager, is my friend. She'll heat it up. Enough, go to sleep now. And I'll go. We'll be working in the orchard tomorrow.

She closed the door tightly after herself, and I was left in the darkness. I sat and looked through the wide dim glass, behind which twisted trunks of old trees emerged in marvellous and phantasmagorical patterns. Early the next morning I noticed a huge orchard on the opposite side of the house where yellow pears, red apples and purple plums hung like colorful lanterns. All the way down near the other houses, the harvest had been gathered. I laid down on the trestle bed with my clothes on, stretched out my tired legs with pleasure. Now, having changed my angle of vision, I saw the dark sky above, stars pulsating in it like fish in a net. They danced in circular patterns, closing in and moving away, now pulling out their tentacles, now rolling them up in a small shiny ball. In complete silence you could hear the house filling up with nocturnal sounds, the wooden walls of the veranda creaked as it got colder, mice scuttered about somewhere up above, from time to time apples fell from the trees in the orchard. On the veranda you could smell the fragrance of dried herbs, walnuts lay on old newspapers spread over the floor, and strings of mushrooms hung down all over the walls. I was absorbing sounds and scents like a sponge. They were new, unusual and therapeutic, like medicine. I was even able to take in a chestful of air – before, it felt as if my chest were filled with needles.

...Stars drew close to my window and pressed toward it, opened up like cheerful children's faces. I couldn't smile yet. I just waved my hand at them and closed my eyes....

6.

The morning seeped into the veranda in a fine milky trickle. The orchard was knee deep in fog that was slowly sinking down and soaking into the earth, making it soft and moist. I opened my eyes and saw the same view above me as yesterday: the old woman was standing over me. But today she was holding a mug of milk in her hand and a plate with crepes – triangular shaped ones stuffed with cottage cheese, they were yellow because of real home cooking oil and eggs.

Having noticed that I woke up, the grandmother carefully put all this splendor on a broken chair.

"Here, have some and then come out into the orchard. We'll be taking off apples from the trees. It's time."

It was good that she left because I flung myself at the crepes like a wolf and nearly choked on the milk.

There was no need to either dress or brush my hair. I went out to the orchard through the veranda door and was filled with admiration: I've never seen such fruit before! Tree branches bent to the ground under the weight of huge apples. The fruit was "with fat cheeks" that looked like the heads of chubby cherubs. The old woman brought a whole pile of woven baskets and placed them under the trees. Now I understood why she said "take off" the apples – they were so juicy that you had to take them carefully because the juice would gush out under the slightest touch. Being freed from their heavy burden, the tree branches shot up gratefully, bowing their crowns.

After we were done with the apples, the time came to pick plums. They were just as juicy, huge, and incredible. It seemed they were powdered with silver dust. You had just to wipe it off, and the plum would flash out in your hand like a purple lantern. The plums were as sweet as honey. No, even sweeter than honey.... I tried to work fast, but the grandmother was always ahead of me. I was barely finishing with one tree when she was done with two. We took full baskets to the veranda and poured the fruits into a large aluminum tray; they still needed to be wiped and laid out. We sorted apples into three types: ones that hadn't grown too ripe went to the cellar, bruised apples were sliced and put on windowsills all over the house, and the grandmother picked some to make juice.

We worked almost till evening. When I looked around the orchard, I noticed that the colors were no longer there – we had undressed it naked. The autumn made its home out there. Only a lonely quince towered above at the end of the orchard. I pointed at it, and the old woman waved her hand:

"It can be like that till November. The fruit will get even sweeter."

After we finally had come inside the house, it seemed like I found myself in paradise – fruits were everywhere, their fragrance made my head swim.

"I'll go over to the *Silpo*," the old woman said, "and you should have some rest. I can see that you're not used to work. And you shouldn't wander around the village – eyes and ears are everywhere there. People will say that I've taken on a hired laborer...."

She didn't seem tired at all. She took off her apron and quickly went down the path that led to the village center.

Left alone, I sat next to the window and stared at the quince tree. About five to seven small yellow lanterns hung on each black branch. A gentle breeze raised a light cheesecloth curtain over the opened door. A red chicken looked through it, cackling loudly, as if expressing its dissatisfaction with the world, a little kitten jumped onto my lap and started purring despairingly, its cold nose dabbed my palm, demanding that I pet her. Something was boiling in a large pot on the gas-stove. Maybe a friend of that red chicken.... I thought: "quin-ce...."

7.

I didn't realize (oh, I was far from there yet!) that some kind of new meaning, unknown to me before, could enter my life through gazing at the orchard. You just look at the trees through the window every day. I have never before seen how one season gives way to the next. And here, in this small village, walled off from the world by mountains, I saw a real miracle for the first time. Just yesterday it was summer in the orchard, heavy with fruits, saturated with all the colors, and today it stood clean and clear, like an operating room or a ballroom before a ball, and the next day I opened my eyes to see winter entering this clear, empty space. It was barely noticeable – a slight shadow darted amid bare trunks. But it was enough to feel its chilly breath. A long period in between seasons was ahead of us, but I swear, three seasons were imprinted in the veranda window in one day, just like in a movie! Would I have noticed it before? Probably not.... Something happened not only to my hearing and voice, but also to my vision. Everything sharpened, and that, which I never used to notice, emerged before me like an epiphany and revelation. But the meaning of human relations was lost to me. The meaning was a spark, shimmering in the darkness. It flares up suddenly and dies away likewise all of a sudden. When it looms in the distance – we move, we're happy, we feel the taste, we try to reach it, grab it, hold it. When it dies away – everything dies with it. Physiological needs of the body become more important. Sometimes it seems that life becomes easier and simpler. But also... more terrible. This period of darkness and indifference ends in insanity or chaos. And if it lasts too long, you degenerate or... become a cynic. A beggar-cynic is a complete villain, a rich man cynic is a mechanism for the satisfaction of needs.

But I was lucky: I was alone with nature, and it never lets you slip.

...The grandmother always woke me up at six. We worked together all day long, and in the evening we spent half an hour sitting on the threshold in silence (I saw night entering the yard), and then I went to bed. The grandmother also turned on the black-and-white TV in her room, and I could hear Mexican melodies from a TV series. Time disappeared. The past hung over my head like a cast iron ball by a thin thread, but for some reason it, this thread, would not break. If it had broken, the ball would have crushed me.... I guess I had to live.

8.

The hut that had become my refuge was higher up than the rest. The village was inhabited by elderly people for whom it was not an easy thing to go all the way up. That's why quite some time passed before I saw anyone. Once a month the old woman's friend paid her a visit – she was lean, bent over with age, and agile just like the grandmother. It was Yakivna, the bathhouse manager.

On seeing me, she flung up her arms:

"Good God! Who is that devil? Where did she come from?"

"God only knows!" My hostess answered, "she came from the woods...."

"Did you tell Petrovych?"

"Don't you know our Petrovych? He's already dead drunk in the morning. And why tell him? He'll destroy the stray, just like they destroyed Ielanum...."

During this conversation I sat on a stool in the middle of the room, turning my head and trying to understand what they were talking about, and how that visit threatened me. My heart fluttered like a small flag in the wind.

"We must have scared her," Yakivna observed, "look how she's breathing...."

"Come, join us," the grandmother called me, "have some tea with us...."

"She needs a bath...," the bathhouse manager observed, "and look what's with her head! The hairdo is just like Ignacio's from *Tropicaliente*!"[25]

"Not Ignacio's, but Juan Carlos'!"

"You're confusing them. Carlos is a millionaire, he can't have hair like that!" Yakivna said confidently, "and Ignacio is that beggar with whom Maria's in love!"

The old women started to quarrel at the top of their voices. Insulted, Yakivna was getting ready to go home. I looked at both with agitation.

"Where are you going, Yakivna?" My hostess said peacefully, "what about tea?"

Yakivna frowned, but she took her seat and started to examine me again.

"Here," she said at last, offering me a cookie.

Resting their elbows on the table, both friends watched me eat.

"You know what," Yakivna finally said, "although she's a stray, she's still a girl, after all! Bring her to my place tomorrow. Closer to nightfall. I'll heat the water – we'll give her a bath. Maybe we'll take her over to Petrovych then – he's still the authority. What if somebody is looking for her?..."

I stopped chewing on the cookie and waved my head in desperation....

"No!" My hostess said resolutely, "God gave her – so it is for God to decide what we should do next! That's enough with what happened to Ielanum, my heart still bleeds for him. We notified them about him – and then what? Was he of any trouble to anyone here? He was a messenger. Truly I'm saying to you – a saint... Maybe this stray came in place of him?..."

"Yes, I feel sorry for Ielanum...," Yakivna sighed and turned to me, "Do you know Ielanum?"

---

25   A Brazilian soap opera that originally was filmed in 1994 and which later was dubbed for showing in the USSR.

That name alarmed me. The combination of those sounds made my eyes burn. His name sounded sad and anxious like a coded phrase, like the name of the abyss, like the howl of a lonely beast. It had nothing human in it.

"She doesn't know him! Let the girl alone! Don't you see, she's not herself...," my old woman said.

And they started to talk about that mysterious Ielanum. I listened attentively, trying to make out what they were saying....

9.

...He was found fifteen years ago in the den of a bear. Before that, a few times locals had seen a weird creature in the woods that moved on all fours but had no fur or tail. A creature with the agility of a monkey following a big brown female bear. "A werewolf!" The villagers decided and stopped hunting in that area. The bear didn't do any harm. What's more – it was under protection of the law that forbade killing rare animals.

...Then times changed. A private restaurant was built down by the road, and the owner included an expensive dish on the menu – bear meat steak. For one carcass he paid a great —for that region – amount of money. And the locals didn't have much money. It was then the time for that bear came. Seven villagers armed with picks and knives (many had already handed in their weapons to the police) set forth in search of the bear's den. Before that, everyone stopped by the church and silently asked God to deliver him from the first blow.

It was winter. The bear was sleeping in its lair. They smoked it out of there, sticking torches into the opening, tried to wake it up with cries and clanking of the lids from camp kettles. Finally, it slowly came out of its shelter with a threatening roar and rose up on its hind legs, blocking the entrance with its body. "Together!" The leader of the group ordered, and seven sharpened picks were stuck into the chest of the two-meter tall animal. The bear took a few steps and fell down, so that the picks pierced it through under the weight of its body. They stuck out of its back, making it look like some kind of mythical beast.

And then they found the "werewolf" inside the lair. He was lying in a deep hollow, which still preserved the warmth of the bear's body, and howled quietly. When that strange creature was dragged outside and thrown next to the bear, around which a red blood stain was already spreading out, turning the snow into a cherry froth, the "werewolf" threw back his head and a weird sound was heard in the air: "Ii-ee-la-a-nu-um!.."

They put the bear onto a cart and carried it to the village. They covered the creature with a sheepskin overcoat and put him next to the bear. On their way back, they dropped him off at a local dispensary. A paramedic and an elderly nurse worked there. Having examined the patient, they concluded that it was a human being. Just grown wild. He probably attached himself to the bear, which lost its babies, and the bear raised him. How many years the man spent in the woods, where he was from, and what his age was – remained a mystery. At first the creature strove to go outdoors and howled drearily. He was called Ielanum, which resembled the sound escaping from his throat. No one took any interest in this finding for seven years. Ielanum lived in the dispensary. They taught him to put on linen pants and a shirt, to eat out of a soup plate, and to sleep in bed. The locals took turns cooking for him. At times, they went to the dispensary as if in their Sunday best or as if they were going to church, with the whole family, and then they watched him eat through the window. They noticed: that visiting the "sprite" brought them luck: cattle recovered from disease, a long-expected letter from relatives arrived from the city... The old paramedic, who missed research, worked with Ielanum every day and recorded his responses in a thick book. More often than not, Ielanum sat on his bed, looking through the window.

In winter, when the scene of the bear killing ran through his mind, he howled at the moon dreadfully and in despair.

And then journalists started coming over to the village. At first – from the local mass media, then from the capital, and later from the foreign press. Ielanum hid from the camera flashes and video cameras, growling threateningly.

One day a green van arrived in the village. By order from above, they were supposed to take Ielanum to the capital for testing. The public gathered around the dispensary, the "sprite" struggled in the hands of the brawny hospital attendants, the paramedic cried, trying to wrest his ward from the grasp of the sadists. When Ielanum grew exhausted and quiet, they hurled him into the back of the van.

The van drove off. The villagers could hear his last cry for a rather long time: "I-i-i-e-e-e-la-a-a...." Since then no one has heard anything about him.

Although, around three years ago, on the TV program *View*, there was an episode about a strange person who lived in an asylum somewhere in... Bashkiria. A physician from that place informed on TV that the man had been raised by a mother bear. And despite living among people for a long time, he never managed to learn either to speak or understand others. When scientific interest in the phenomenon of nature was lost, he was housed there, among the old and poor. While speaking, the doctor stroked the patient's dishevelled head, and the man's lifeless gaze was fixed on the camera. One of the villagers saw that episode and later, having gathered a crowd near the *Silpo* store, he insisted that the man was their Ielanum....

...His name is the wind in the field, the name-howl in which there is more sense than in people's chattering.

Ielanum does not like words and he will never find himself company. Words are leeches that fill your mouth with bitterness.

Ielanum was pushed into the world, and the world did not accept him.

Ielanum looks at life from the depth of the well and sees only a round spot of bright light above him and understands nothing in the rushing shadows around him.

Ielanum builds his own world – within him.

Ielanum does not make anyone love him.

No one loves Ielanum – he arouses fear and aversion.

Ielanum's loneliness is not warmed by any thread of light, by any random bird that could have brought a twig in its beak onto the treetop of his loneliness.

Ielanum's loneliness is endless.

Ielanum makes his way from darkness into darkness – light frightens him.

Ielanum is the light of light and the darkness of darkness: he cannot be caught in either of those.

No one addresses him. No one calls him – and that is why the world does not turn.

Ielanum is one, who chose to become insane.

10.

...At night I couldn't fall asleep for a long time. I dreamt about the "sprite." Who abandoned him in the forest and when, who betrayed him? Why would he need this world, this asylum in a foreign land?

In the morning, when the stars began to burst like soap bubbles in a sky turned gray, I felt my head begin to ache. Rather, my skin and even my hair.

I tried to run all five fingers through it and I encountered solid oakum. What is it? I looked at myself in the window and sank back against the pillow: a monster was looking back at me through the silhouettes of the trees. Stiff rods of tangled hair stuck up every which way. My scalp hurt unbearably. I didn't feel it at all before. I pulled at the strands in vain until I noticed a pair of scissors on the windowsill. They were rusty. I haphazardly started to cut the strands. When the work was done, the sun was already up. And I felt better. Insomuch that I was able to shuffle off my sweater and dirty jeans for the first time. How could I have been in them for so long? Now I felt that not only did my scalp hurt, but also the skin of my entire body. It felt as if it had been stripped off my body – even a slight motion caused incredible burning pain. But a little later it abated. I sat on the bed stark naked, listening to my body.

The grandmother came in, bringing, as always, a mug of milk. On seeing my pulled hair, she looked at me suspiciously:

"What is that you did? Did you go into a rage or what?"

I flattened my hair down and the grandmother calmed down:

"Oh, I see, you were fixing it up?! That's good. One has to be tidy. Should we go to the bathhouse?"

I nodded. I moved my dirty clothes aside.

"I see. Let's find something for you to wear. And this," the old woman nodded toward my rags, "we'll wash them today. The weather is nice, it'll be dry until the evening."

She took my jeans and sweater, and before taking them away, she went through my pockets with an overt curiosity. She took out a bunch of keys, a bundle of money, and a white business card out of there.... We both looked at these things with surprise.

"Does it all belong to you?" The old woman finally uttered in a trembling voice. "Who are you? Should I notify anyone about you or what? What a riddle you've given me, girl.... What should I do with you?"

She carefully put all the things she found in a plastic bag and put them away in a drawer.

"Fine, we'll figure it out. Here, put this on!" She rummaged through the drawer and threw me an old cotton robe and somebody's worn-out shoes onto the bed. "Wear it for now. And I'll go wash your things. What if you're some kind of princess and I'm keeping you here in filth.... Not good. We'll go have a bath in the evening."

I put on the robe. It had a moldy odor, but it was pleasant to feel my own body and understand that I would soon wash off all the dirt which, it seemed, had been ingrained in every single cell of my body.

In an hour or an hour and a half, the old woman dropped in again.

"There, work is done. Now let's cut your hair properly."

She was holding a hair trimmer in her hand. I shuddered and waved my hands in panic.

"Don't be afraid, this machine is for cutting hair. My son brought it over one day when we used to have sheep.... Come on, sit down. You've got a thing here that can only be cut with a trimmer!"

I had to listen to her. I obediently moved my head up to her. Metal teeth began to snap, biting into the shag. It hurt. And then it was cold. When the grandmother finished the job, I ran my hand over my head – it was completely bald.

"Stay here until the evening," the old woman ordered, "and I'll go to Yakivna and ask her not to close the bathhouse and save the water. We have a problem with hot water – we don't have enough for everyone.... If you want to go out – go to the orchard. And nowhere else. You'll freeze."

She wrapped up the shorn locks in a newspaper and went to bury them in the garden....

11.

I lay down on the bed again and felt how good it was to lie under a blanket without my clothes on. From time to time I touched my head and that feeling was pleasant. I started dozing off. And then something happened that never happened again after that even after my mind had cleared up. Not even now....

At first it seemed as if somebody had sat down on one end of my bed – it even sagged a bit. Then – a hand.... It stroked my face so tenderly that I didn't dare open my eyes and kept quiet, holding my breath. The hand and breath I felt were so real, so familiar.... Then somebody embraced me over the blanket, cuddled me like a baby, and his warm lips warmed my blazing ear.... I caught a barely audible voice: "I will love you for a long time.... Forever.... I miss you so much...." It was not a dream, or delusion, or sickly imagination. I felt all the heaviness of the body, the strength of the embrace, the scent of tobacco. Now I realize it was a phantom, materialized by my desire. Even when a sound coming from the woods made me shudder and come back from that dimension, the indentation on the bed next to me was warm....

...When the sun fell behind the horizon, my hostess took me down to the village to the bathhouse. Before that, she put a quilted coat on me and wrapped my head in a coarse woollen kerchief. We came down a narrow trail to the main (and only) street. The houses stood submerged in the dusk, their whitewashed walls were seemingly illuminated by a blue flame from inside. The yards were empty. The day was over. I kept looking down, just watching my steps, as if I were going to the scaffold.

Our guest from yesterday was already waiting for us near a half-ruined fence that surrounded the building with no windows. It was the bathhouse.

"Hurry up – the water's getting cold!" Yakivna said, taking me into the shower room.

What did they want from me? What should I do?

Noticing my helplessness, both old women quickly pulled the quilted coat, shoes, the robe, and kerchief off me and placed me under a faucet. Yakivna turned the knob of the faucet, and a thin trickle of water came out.

"Here, take some soap," my grandmother said, "wash yourself thoroughly!"

And she showed me how to do it. I followed her movements. While I was sloppily lathering myself, both grandmothers stood not very far from me in a similar pose:

with one elbow propped up on the other hand. Cosmic sadness glimmered in their eyes.

"God forbid," one finally uttered, "just skin and bones...."

Soapsuds foamed beneath my feet, gurgling out into the grid of a water drain. I scrubbed myself as hard as I could till those soapy streams became clear. There was no more water left.

"That's it!" The bathhouse manager said, "There's no water left.... Receive the client!" She gave a cheerful wink at my hostess, and the latter quickly enwrapped me in a large sheet that we had brought over. Then she took my clothes out of the plastic bag.

"Everything is clean. You can put it on now."

Then, in complete darkness, we set off to Yakivna's house that was located nearby.

After the stifling bathhouse it was pleasant to have some fresh air, and it was even more pleasant to find myself in a house where a table that had been set earlier awaited us – jam, apples, potato and cheese stuffed pastries in a large pot, wrapped in towels. The house was similar to ours – the same apples, plums, and walnuts laid out on the windowsills, strings of dried mushrooms, an old TV set, covered with a faded velvet cloth, a round table in the middle of the room....

Yakivna put pastries out in a soup plate, their reddish sides glistened as if they were wax figures. Sitting us at the table, Yakivna fetched a bottle out of the buffet – it was almost black, covered in so much dust as if it had been there for about twenty years. She didn't happen to have either wineglasses or shot glasses, for that reason she put large potbelly mugs in front of us. My grandmother winked at me:

"It's her famous blackberry wine. Yakivna is a master of this craft!"

"No way! Everything is in the past now. Only leftovers remain," Yakivna replied, thoroughly concealing the pleasure of being praised. "People used to come to me to buy a bottle from all the districts, especially during the summer or fall, when there were a lot of tourists. At first I used to sell near the *Silpo* store, and later they began to look for me themselves.... Now I've already forgotten the recipe...."

She carefully wiped the bottle with a rag, pulled out the cork with a delicious sound, and poured out the wine in the mugs. It was black and thick like honey. Or blood....

The very same black and thick darkness flooded the house from outside. The night pressed tightly against the window, watching us with a few yellow eyes. The light bulb was barely glowing above the table. All this produced the impression of the last supper, of some kind of ritual. I took off the kerchief and, I suppose, my bald head shone in that twilight like a paper lantern, lit from the inside. My hostess looked at me and flung her arms up:

"Just look at her – a pure angel!"

"A handsome girl," Yakivna agreed, "If only you could fatten her up a bit.... Here, drink some – maybe you'll work up an appetite," she passed me a mug, "take a look at how many pastries are here!"

I took the mug carefully in my hand and saw a reflection of my eye in the black circle of the poured wine.... I took a sip....

12.

And what wine it was! The first drop was like blistering viscid resin. Sweet and thick lava flowed down my throat, its stream ran further, washing off all my insides. It was as if I saw myself from inside, felt my every cell – just like I did in the morning and.... I lost feeling in my legs. It was as if a butterfly-swallowtail was trying to open its glued wings inside my chest. The thick liquid had the taste of time – the bitterness of twenty-year-old dust ingrained into the glass of the bottle, the roughness of the wild berries that died long ago, and the sweetness of yellow sugar (a kind that no longer can be found!). And also – a particular aroma of some kind of unknown potion. My lips nestled eagerly on the mug, and I tore myself away only when they had turned black and when whiteness glimmered on the bottom.

The grandmothers watched me with interest, nodding their heads affectionately. With no less curiosity did I look at them as if I were seeing them for the first time. Under the dingy parasol of light, they resembled two trees that stood motionless in freezing weather. White kerchiefs accentuated the old age of their skin and its extreme ancientness. They've lived here for a hundred years, or even longer. Compassion emanated from their clear eyes. A hot wave reached the tips of my feet and, rising up, it rolled back. When it got to the level of my chest, it seemed as if it were washing off the needles that were stuck in my heart and lungs. I tried to control myself, but in a minute the wave was blazing in my throat, then – it started roaring in my head in search of an escape. I didn't know what to do, so I took my head in my hands. My head was humming and splitting until a hot flood of tears finally burst through. I was crying and laughing at the same time. I felt better with every moment as if I were driving snakes, lizards, black mice, and slithery rats out of myself. That was the impression I had....

When I came to my senses, I saw that my hostess was clasping my head to her sunken breast, wiping tears from my face with the white end of a kerchief.

...I haven't cried ever since. And not because I feel ashamed or too proud. I just can't....

The grandmothers nodded to each other as if they had done a very important deed.

"So, what is your name? Maybe now you'll tell us?" My hostess asked, stroking my head (her palm absorbed my fear like a sponge).

"Angelika...."

I didn't recognize my voice. As well as that name, that had to become mine from then on. It was strange to me. It belonged to somebody else. It was fake like the breasts of a Hollywood beauty....

13.

I lived with grandmother Hanna Tarasivna (that was her name) till midwinter. If not for Petrovych – a man of unpleasant appearance with glassy eyes – I would have stayed longer. For some reason, Petrovych decided to walk about his dominion. It was good that our house was on the hill, and we saw through the window that he was slowly walking up our path, like a giant bug that crawls up a stem. His hairy nostrils were dilating, and his boozy face was taking on a red beet tint with every step. Petrovych was a king and a god here: only old people were left in the village, and he regularly collected taxes from them in the form of home-distilled spirits and food.

I hid myself on the veranda and remained there until he left. Hanna Tarasivna wined and dined him.

"He won't come back anymore. At least not till spring," she said, "I poured a bucket of water onto the path, it will soon freeze, and it won't be that easy to get here!"

But I realized: it was time! And I started to prepare for a journey. It made Hanna Tarasivna upset, but she didn't talk me out of it. She took a bag with money, the business card and the keys out of the drawer. I left half of the money in the drawer despite all her objections, and I put what remained – and there was not much left – in the pocket of my jeans. I had to take an old sheepskin overcoat and put on a pair of thick wool socks, which Hanna Tarasivna had knitted over a couple of days, under my sneakers.

"Where will you go?" She sighed the entire time.

And I realized that I HAD to go, as if the runic inscription "Road" fell to my lot out of the sleeve of the sky.... I couldn't know then, that winter, in a small mountain village, which shows up neither on maps nor in pictures (as no one has ever taken pictures of it) that, sooner or later, that runic inscription would fall to my lot anyway.

...I left the Hut that Stood on a Hill three days after the visit of the district police officer. Hanna Tarasivna woke up early, cooked *tokan*,[26] fried crepes, and put half of that breakfast in my backpack.

We went out to the orchard together. All covered in hoarfrost, it glistened; you could drink the air like spring water.

"Everyone in this life bears his cross," the old woman said, "The more mistakes you make, the heavier the cross becomes. And yours, my child, is really small. Bear it, endure, and have faith...."

She embraced me, kissed me three times, and made the sign of the cross over me.

I had to walk through the sleepy village, to go down the valley, to walk past a mountain and a bit through the woods. According to Hanna Tarasivna, there was a highway there with buses going to the regional center and to the railway station.

It was still dark outside. The icy fog wreathed like milk before me. I walked five or six meters and turned around: there was nothing behind me. There was no grandmother, no orchard, no house there – everything dissolved in the white haze.... I felt sharp pain in my heart for the first time in several months. I realized: life has no taste, in its pure form it's like distilled water. We add salt, pepper, or sugar to it ourselves. When life acquires taste – your heart hurts more.

At first I had only one reason to disappear. Then I realized that there could be many more reasons like that. For example, a desire to learn how some people are different from others. In appearance? In belonging to this

---

26   An old traditional Transcarpathian dish.

or that race? In the contents of their wallet? In the degree of education or standard of culture? Everything was that way.

But I wanted to understand how I, precisely, how I am different from any other person – from hundreds of people! – during such moments such as when I want to eat, to sleep, when I am cold, when I have a toothache or headache, when I am alone.... So far my experience was telling me – I am no different.

The hut dissolved like a sugar cube in hot milk. I could have never learned that it existed. With the scent of dried fruits, with the taste of polenta – *tokan*, with this grandmother, exacting and lonely. She had never known another world where you didn't have to wake up at four o'clock in the morning and work hard every day. But that other world, in fact, was not worth a single wrinkle on her wise forehead....

I stood for a minute, peering to see her woollen kerchief emerge from the fog, and then I turned around and quickly walked down the slope. The road didn't frighten me. It started with a bright point of pain just as everything real should start.

In a few hours when I approached the highway, I slipped my hand into my pocket and took a set of keys out of it. I closed it in my hand and waited until the metal had warmed up.... Then I threw it far away. They clanked in the air and silently fell in the snow....

If I ever get tired of life, if I have a choice where to end my days, I will come back here. Even if I live in a different corner of the world....

PART FOUR

1.

...Girls are lolling on a couch watching *Amarcord* on a VCR. I can't imagine where they got such an antique. Once (in a different life) I myself used to look for Fellini in video shops, but in vain. And apparently they found him. There probably are those kind of places preserved in time in this industrial town where you can find anything.

I'm partially catching the movie, imagining its heroes and, importantly, submerging myself in an atmosphere of the prewar provincial Italy of Fellini's-Guerra's childhood – with poplar wool, fog, and a boyish yearning for love. I'm listening while cleaning glazed tiles in the kitchen. Then I turn on the vacuum cleaner. The girls grumble something discontentedly and close the door. It doesn't insult me. Quite the opposite – I'm happy. The question "what will be tomorrow?" doesn't bother me. I understand that "tomorrow" is today that hasn't come yet. It's always a few steps away from "now." And that's why there is no reason to be afraid. If I breathe, live, move now – that's already good enough. No birds, animals, or trees think about tomorrow?...

The girls' names are Lucy and Vira. I clean, wash, scrub. They are the ones in charge. They turn on the tape player and tell me to go to my room. Their mother is a wonderful woman who picked me up at the railway station after a lengthy amount of time living in the attics of high-rise buildings and on hard benches at the railway station. I became a dog and she, my owner, picked me up. She wasn't afraid to pick me up.

For (as it turned out later) before her present-day life, she used to pick up dogs off the street and to nurse them back to health. Then she gave them to "good hands." It was up until she got happily married. This happiness for her became the beginning of the end of her love for dogs. I was the last period in this epic. And our encounter was the last day of her crisis, after which she decided to live happily. Just the way she got married.

She came to the railway station. She was wearing wonderful perfumes and a luxurious mink coat that looked like the golden fleece – strange, strange – and she sat on a shabby stool next to me. She could have gone to any hotel, but she came here. By force of habit. I didn't have that habit. I was always a successful girl and didn't know what it was to go railway stations.... The train has left the station!

I was now sitting at the railway station in ragged jeans and grandmother's sheepskin overcoat, realizing that the only true thing in my life was the road, the change of faces and impressions – a kaleidoscope of feelings, for the sake of which I came to this world. It was as if I had jumped into a mirror and emerged from its other side – with silver amalgam on my skin. It was all the same to me that I was shivering with cold.

"You're probably hungry?" The woman in golden fleece asked me suddenly. In fact I did want to eat – something hot. The last thing I ate was an unfinished sandwich in a railway station cafe. It reeked of somebody's filthy fingers. And of fish. By then, I became used to being simpler. Much simpler.

"Yes," I answered.

And the woman took me to a restaurant near the railway station. She ordered a luxurious dinner – crabmeat salad, chopped meat with vegetables, julienne, and wine.

And I was forced to listen to a long story of love and hate. When I just started listening, I realized: this woman isn't able to master the road. She wanted to wear golden fleece and to buy sets of china. And stray dogs didn't fit in the range of these whims. And yet, when she said that she could take me in, I wagged my tail. I had to rest for a while.

"You have such powerful energy," the woman said.

We stayed at the restaurant till it closed. I was incredibly warm. Sometimes it's worth feeling such warmth – a bit of warmth and a little satiation. These are such simple things....

The woman brought me into this luxurious house – with two children and a stout husband, whom I saw only two or three times a week.

And here I am now washing, scrubbing, cleaning. And listening to the melody flowing out of the tape player....

And it is just the continuation of my journey. And I love it.

2.

This house is too big even for a family of four. In my opinion, it's immense. I clean three large halls, four bedrooms, and two huge living rooms – studios. And this is apart from the bathrooms and a spacious kitchen that a chef from a local restaurant runs every morning. There are also "entresols," and one has to go up steep stairs to get there. These are two narrow room-compartments, and I live in one of them. The other one is obviously for another maid. Maybe for a nanny or, to put it better, a *bonne*.

The atmosphere here is electrified. The sixteen and seventeen year old girls hate their father. They hate him, yet they are afraid of him, and they remove their makeup every time before he comes back home. They hate their father, and they seem to despise their mother. The husband and wife have been tired of each other for a long time now. The impression is as if the corpse of love is decomposing in the middle of a luxurious hall. That's why it's so stifling here. But nobody feels it. Everyone is preoccupied with themselves....

Sooner or later, people who don't feel any love turn into a zombie, into amorphous nothingness, they are not satisfied with life no matter how good it is.

In the morning when the host entered the kitchen, I wanted to turn invisible. He never said hello and never glanced in my direction. He simply ordered: "Coffee. No sugar." And he fenced himself off with a newspaper. The hostess appeared only when the door was closed behind him and when one could hear the swish of his tires outside. She, too, had coffee and gazed through the window for a long time. And then, having shed her drowsiness, she dictated a list of things for me to do that day. It was long. It would be easier for me to do my work if there were more warmth in that home.

Everything is different upstairs, in the "entresols," where I go at the end of the day, all worn out: soft evening light flows through a simple cotton curtain that makes my room resemble a jar of translucent honey. It's so nice to sleep in here. An old oak tree towers outside my window; it's almost right above my bed (the roof is sloped a bit like that of a mansard). At times, when the wind rises at night, it tosses an acorn in my window, and I wake up. Then, not understanding where I am, I can't fall asleep for a long time....

It seems to me that I'm on the veranda in a Godforsaken village, and tenderness makes my heart shrink. I plunge into the aura of scents, into blunted nocturnal sounds, into a neonatal state – with a light and easy void, the inside of which, little by little, is filling up with new sensations. At one moment I shudder, jump up in order to escape from police whistles....

...My thoughts are racing, I can't gather them. Once again I'm fearful of the recurrence of the illness. I bandaged myself with an overly tight and impenetrable cocoon....

Life has always appeared to me as a contingency. And even now I believe that one has to bless only one day that begins outside the window and not think too much about the next two!

Everything that I had been building up in my imagination was destroyed in just one instant – a cosy home, journeys, a sea of flowers on a windowsill, a library put together with love, a dog and a cat, pictures on the walls, movies for the two of us to watch, music, rain, snow, New Year's holidays, a fireplace, crisp bed sheets, and, of course, the pleasant heaviness of a baby in my crossed arms... It's not easy to realize that it's NEVER going to happen. I'm still not sure where the strength to accept this "never" came from. As I happened to meet people (such as my hostess, for example), who didn't and wouldn't come to terms with this, and they expected certain changes every year. What changes? They themselves were unable to explain it. From the beginning they had the scheme of a happy cloudless existence embedded in them, and to accept the fact that reality couldn't fit in it like in a procrustean bed was beyond their understanding. I quoted Mandelstam's[27] words that he once spoke to his wife: "Who told you that you MUST be happy?! Seriously, who? And is happiness only in "whistling like a nightingale" one's whole life away?

In April the couple went for a holiday to Greece. Before that, tranquility reigned in the house. As if before the storm. And it drew near as soon the door closed after the hosts.

The girls immediately took to their phones non-stop, gathering their friends together. And within an hour, I received a great number of orders that made my head spin. To tell the truth, panicking about the scope of the event I even wanted to call their parents. But then I decided to give in.

On their first day of freedom, the girls did not go to the lyceum, responding to all my coaxing with loud laughter, in which one could sense something ominous. And I was not mistaken. In the evening the house was overcrowded with people. Earlier I did think that the girls had led a quite turbulent life outside this little nest. By the beginning of the party, my young wards turned into real vamps (though,

---

27   The great Russian poet Osip Mandelstam (1891-1938), who was imprisoned and executed by Stalin.

both were delicate blondes with quite inexpressive faces): with their eyes lavishly made up, blood-red lips, and sophisticatedly styled hair.

In addition to making sandwiches, I also had to welcome guests in the vestibule. Some strangers, who were much older than the sisters, dumped their jackets and coats on my arms, took bottles out of plastic bags, and went to the living room. When the room was packed with a great many of them and gray cigarette smoke hung thick in the room, the doorbell rang again. By that time, the guests were dancing, making out in every corner, sitting or lying on the carpet, and music resounded all over the house. And I sat by the coat rack next to the door, trying to make sure no one of the guests sneaked anything out of the house. I imagined with horror how much work awaited me after the party was over. And would it ever be over?

So, the doorbell rang. I answered it.

The new visitor was not like the rest of them. He was wearing a nice white coat, was perfectly shaven, with an indifferent and ironic air. For some reason I understood at once, everything had been organized for him. He didn't bring a bottle.

He took his time entering, watching me hang his coat. I became disaccustomed to being looked at. I didn't look at myself in the mirror for a long time and I was sure that emptiness would be reflected there.

"I've seen you somewhere...," the guest said and unceremoniously took me by my chin, "are you wearing a wig?"

I shrugged my shoulders, not understanding what he wanted from me. My hair had grown out and stuck up like a fluffy hat over my head, and really did look like a wig. I shook my head and tore away from him. It was a good thing that Vira darted out into the vestibule with Lucy following her. They grabbed the guest and took him to the room. Immediately silence ensued in there. The guest must have been an important person. I suspect that they bet whether he would come. And my girls won.

I decided not to go to bed but stay and do everything possible to control the situation, so I sat myself in the kitchen so that I could see the front door. The guests dropped in from time to time to order sandwiches and to request beer, vodka, ice, and champagne.

At midnight I leaned my head on the table and almost dozed off when that guest entered the kitchen. He had a fairly unkempt appearance. He looked around the kitchen.

"Nice house...."

I couldn't keep up the conversation. In general, I hadn't quite yet gotten used to talking.

The guest sat opposite me, carpingly staring in my face.

"I've seen you somewhere."

I was in front of his eyes, like a leaf, lying on the glass under the eye-piece of a microscope – I even felt the molecules rushing in a chaotic Brownian motion inside me. Once again he took me by the tip of my chin and turned my face left and right. I jerked back, knocking over a little basket with bread sitting on the table. And when I lifted it beneath that gaze, he sat smiling contentedly, lighting up his cigarette.

"I remember now. You see green eyes like that just once in a lifetime...."

He puffed a wisp of smoke and made a telling pause, disturbing impulses were streaming out of his cold eyes.

"I saw your picture on the subway when I visited the capital... I don't think I'm mistaken, I have a good memory for faces. Somebody is looking for you."

I couldn't, couldn't speak....

"And you," he continued, "you don't want to be found. Interesting...."

I wanted to get up and leave, but he grabbed me by my hand and sat me down.

"So, you've done something. But what?..."

Holding me by my hand, he moved closer. I could barely stand his touch. Not just because he was impudent and persistent, I was in the dimension where any human touch would provoke aversion. I could pet dogs, hold a cat in my hands, feed the fish and birds, I'd survive if a rat or a grass snake crawled on my chest, but somebody else's touch made me feel dizzy. Darkness was flooding my brain. He lightly shook me by my shoulders:

"There-there.... Why worry so much? Everything can be worked out amicably. Take it easy.... I won't eat you...."

He said all this with long pauses, and it frightened me even more – his every word seemed significant, as if the stranger knew everything about me.

"I don't really care who you are and where you're from. If you're afraid, it's probably for a reason. I won't look into it." He kept silent for a few seconds. "But if a reason exists, it's easy to find it out. Does it make sense? Especially I," he particularly accentuated that word, "can do it easily."

I-i-i-e-e-e-la-a-a-nu-u-um....

"So," he continued, not knowing who he was dealing with, "it's a fortunate time and place for us to have met. We have to help each other. I suggest: a favor for a favor. What do you say, doll? "

I felt like howling long and protractedly. I felt a flat warm palm stroking my knee, and the aversion to his touch prevented me from understanding what he was saying.

"One word, yes," his hand stopped moving, remaining on my lap like the bottom of a red-hot frying-pan, "I need some of your master's documents. In fact, that's the reason I'm here. I've looked everywhere – there's nothing upstairs! They must be in the safe. I need you to get them for me. And I'll forget about your existence. Okay? Or do you want money? Just let me know – that wouldn't be a problem!"

3.

I should mention one peculiarity here, which I've always had hidden, and which I thought was natural. And now it turned out to be my salvation: everything that I could not and would not accept was blocked by paintings that emerged in my imagination. They were always different. Now, feeling somebody's hand on my shivering knees, I saw something entirely different around me. *An ancient Victorian style room with a fireplace. A chair loomed in the middle of the room in the dusk. A redheaded girl, wearing a green scarf and a red skirt made of glossy satin, was sitting in it with her back to the audience. Bright yellow shadows were pulsing in her braids. I wanted to step closer to see her face. But then I realized it wasn't worth it: I should paint it from this perspective, from the door-step.... And only pure colors should be used. The dim outline of the face across from me was diffusing, almost dissolving in those colors. It was gone. I was wondering who she was, this girl at the fireplace, and why she was alone. Why her companion was not there, in the corner, occupied with her needlework, or why there was no white poodle there or a cage with a parrot in it?*

The painting disappeared only when I felt his lips on my neck. At this moment Vira darted into the room. She had a bellicose air.

"Now it's all clear!" She yelled and swept wineglasses off the table. They splintered. Having heard the noise, Lucy rushed in. They both began to bawl....

I didn't care. I couldn't immerse myself into another abyss of human passions. I got up and headed to my room. As if in a dream, I went up to the "entresols" and went to bed. I had a terrible headache....

Love – it's painful. When it's over – the memory of the body remains, and it makes other, new relations impossible. That's the reason I think now that one has to live alone. Imposing one's will, tastes, complexes, dissatisfaction, mood, and way of life onto somebody else is unnatural! To expect obedience, subordination and a maximum amount of frankness from another person is insidious. I wish I had realized it before....

A long time ago I read a boring novel The French Lieutenant's Woman *by John Fowles. At first I thought it was protracted, too farfetched, and cheesy. The main heroine was dragged by the scruff of the neck into it from a different time: a young woman longs for freedom and goes toward it by means of deception and suffering. Where would such a woman come from in the Victorian era?! Only later I did I understand that artistically depicted time, nature, and history – it was only a frame that the genius novelist used to underscore a single idea. It can be expressed in a single motto: "People, you are free!" But the fear and illusions, instilled though our upbringing, habits, and all that is immanent in humankind, push us toward one another like waves in an ocean. There's no getting around it....*

Sorry, I'm digressing. But then, when I was following the ball unreeling under my feet, I thought many thoughts and learned a lot. The thoughts and pictures emerging in my head did not let me fall into despair.

The more so, since in a few hours after the incident in the kitchen I walked about the city in the hours before dawn – completely free, wearing the same jeans and sheepskin overcoat. Broken down but... happy. A new day was breaking. The acrid scent of dead love no longer touched my sharpened sense of smell.

The city is an amazing sight between three and four in the morning! It stretches like a dark beast with reddish patches on its sides, sighing under its breath in its sleep. A thousand heels don't tear its skin to pieces. It belongs only to itself and to its dreams. I even wanted to laugh. It was a weird and sweet feeling. I entered a public garden, went to the furthest corner and sat on a bench. Trees with little green leaves, which were breaking free, clustered around me from all sides, and the grass pierced through the brown sphere of the earth with a rustle. I dozed off, and when I opened my eyes, it was morning already, and the ground was indeed stitched with thin green threads.

As usual, I washed my face in a bathroom at a railway station. I slipped my hand into my pocket to get a handkerchief and got everything I had out of there. It turned out I had a bit of money left and a plastic card with the name Joshua McLain on it....

The town hadn't fully been purged of its gray color, and I suddenly felt that I really badly wanted other colors. I gave my overcoat to a railway station beggar and bought a third-class train ticket to Crimea....

4.

There's always the odor of boiled eggs in a third-class wagon. People start eating here right after the train begins to move. Newspapers are being spread out, eggs for the entire family are set out on them, and people knock and keep knocking them against the table. An unpleasant odor penetrates the entire space, and the eggshells scrunch under your feet.

Despite the fact that the season had just started, the wagon was crowded with people. I got onto the third top bunk immediately and pulled a thick blanket over my head – I was hiding from those smells, from conversations, and from being looked at.

...The southern town welcomed me with the aroma of coffee and honey, with the cry of seagulls, with a variety of colors and the din of the market. But the most important thing was, of course, the sea! It was somewhere very close, behind a stone balustrade of the seafront – huge, blue-green, all curled with tiny milk-white "baa-lambs." They used to bring me to the sea, usually, to very respectable resorts with ultramarine swimming pools and white hammock chairs, in which I would read books avidly.

This new sea had a particular scent – storm clouds high in the air probably have that scent, and– a milkshake, too. I wanted to dive in it straight away. But first I decided to find a place to stay while I still had some money left.

I turned at random onto a narrow side street that was entwined all around with brown veins of old vines and entered the first yard I came to. It was all entangled with clothes lines and covered with sheets, swimming suits, and towels. A gentle breeze tossed a sheet back, opening up a view of an orchard and a few courtyard houses. A stout elderly woman was sitting by the summer kitchen. That was the landlady. Her name was Maria Hryhorivna. I probably didn't make the impression on her of a person who could be let into the house. She said that all the rooms were taken and there was only a bed left in a small barn. I didn't care. The barn was amazing: tiny golden strings of sunshine hung from small holes in the roof, and sweet-scented armfuls of miscellaneous herbs were drying. In addition, a pile of fresh bed sheets, washed so well that they had a blue hue, was sitting on the bed.

Maria Hryhorivna asked to pay upfront and to give her my passport. I paid for five days. As for the passport, I lied that my parents who were arriving soon had it. Everything was settled.

After the door was closed behind my landlady, I took off my clothes. It was really hot and I wanted to go to the beach as soon as possible. My jeans looked miserable. That's why when I saw a pair of scissors on the table, I cut them off a few inches above the knee. They're shorts now. My ragged shorts went well with my similarly faded tee-shirt. I had nothing else. Some clothes that my hostess gave me in the city were left in the "entresols," I didn't take them. I had very little money left. I took five *hryvnias* and shoved the rest under the blanket. I leapt outside. Maria Hryhorivna cast a sceptical glance at me....

...The sea was like hops. I got drunk after the first time I bathed in it, it seemed as if I had plunged into a huge pool filled with champagne. My brain was buzzing, my cheeks were glowing. I laid down on a round stone. The sea was fizzing and foaming nearby, just like oil in a frying pan. I felt like eating. For the first time.

"Honey baklava! Nuts! Hot homemade oriental dumplings!" could be heard from afar.

I opened my eyes. A woman of wheat-colored complexion with a wicker basket was walking along the shore. I had never bought anything on the street before, it was considered bad manners. I waved my hand and became ashamed of that gesture: it was vulgar to call an elderly woman that way. But she came to me quickly and eagerly, put her basket right under my nose and folded back a snow-white towel. I felt short of breath. A real treasure was put there in orderly batches: diamond-shaped reddish sweet pastries, glazed with honey and sprinkled with powdered sugar. Incredibly delicious and inexpensive! Then I went for a swim again, and the sea licked the sweet syrup off my palms.

I stayed on the beach for a long time. For so long, that I didn't notice that the street lamps had lit up on the seafront. Lilac twilight was rising from behind the mountains, the sun quickly plunged behind the horizon, and streams of incredible odors, which were not perceptible during the day, floated into the town. The scent of wild orchid blended in with another one – a rich scent coming from charcoal grills and huge kettles filled with pilaf. Pilaf and shish kebab were sold right in the street. I bought a plate of pilaf and ate it, sitting on a stone balustrade and watching people. I also watched painters setting up their French easels and painter's cases. I decided to buy paints and paper the next day....

The merry southern night was breaking, life on the seafront was in full swing. The music coming from the restaurants grew louder, and the crowd of vacationers grew and swayed in front of me like a solid multicolored mass. I had to get going. I noticed that, having finished their work, some artists had gathered on the beach under a rock, they were grilling mussels, opening bottles of wine and beer, and, it seemed, were settling there for the night.

After wandering along the streets for a long time, I found the house I was staying in, and when I finally opened the wicket gate, I saw that life was in full swing there as well. A family of four occupied the table and was eating up a great deal of fried bullhead fish, a young couple secluded themselves in a hammock under a wide-branching acacia, men headed by the host settled themselves on stools near the summer kitchen and heatedly played dominoes. Maria Hryhorivna was sitting at the threshold in a large cane chair like a queen. The yard, house, orchard, and the very stout hostess – everything was so different from that other yard, and that other grandmother there, in the mountains....

I said hello but heard no answer. I quickly made my way to my small barn and went to bed with pleasure. I mechanically ran my fingers under the blanket to make sure the money was there. It wasn't there. I rummaged through all the sheets. In vain.

The fact that money was gone did not upset me. It meant only that tomorrow would be a new day with new worries. But I got used to it.

...I don't remember my emotions then at all. Maybe, I didn't have any at all? As I said before, I could easily take a mouse in my hands and I wouldn't scream from touching a sna ke...

EPILOGUE

Joshua McLain

August 2005, San Francisco

1.

Dear Mr. Severyn:

I think Angie will not have a chance to get back to this letter any time soon. That's why I decided to finish it. In order to "put this matter to rest," as they say. To tell the truth, I'm forcing myself to write. The easiest thing for me to do is to "kill" the text. But then, I would feel guilty before Angie. Furthermore, having read what she wrote (I didn't do it on purpose, it happened by coincidence), I just couldn't destroy her words. Since she hoped that you would read them.... Also, I feel I have to clarify something. And I hope you will not bother us anymore after that.

I would like to cut to the chase. But I don't know where to start. I have a good idea of what you must be feeling after you read what my wife has written. But I have to make it clear: it's only what survived in her memory. In reality, it seems to me, everything was much worse.

I have to admit, when I was rereading everything she wrote to you, I could hardly refrain from many emotions. For this reason I apologize for my somewhat uneven style.

So, what happened in reality? I'll start from the end. I found Angie on the Koktebel seafront. I am saying "found" – but I had never looked for her. It was a chance meeting, just as the first one was in the mountains. I can imagine what you must be thinking now....

It was almost impossible to recognize her. Everything she wrote above is a little bit of what actually happened. Her face and body was covered in scars and bruises. You should know it. And I repeat, everything that she wrote, she wrote when she had a chance to live. Now I myself can more clearly understand the essence of this little girl – not to see the evil, with which the world abounds, and time and again I am surprised at your hard-heartedness and I am thankful to God that He brought Angie to me.

Our first meeting looked like this: in front of me, almost on the edge of a cliff that overlooked a picturesque sea of colors – an autumn forest – stood a strange looking creature covered in paint, with a shock of long hair rolled into tubes. I saw her from behind, so it took me a while to figure out if it was a girl or a boy. Her painting drew my attention. And when she turned around, her eyes set me ablaze. Eyes like that are usually painted on icons – large, sad and... empty. You look with unseeing eyes like that at a crowd – at everyone and at no one in particular. I don't know a better way to explain it to you. If an artist, say, Rafael or Vrubel chose a mortal woman as his model, the expression he portrayed came alive. And on canonical canvases – the image is abstract. The faces of saints are unemotional. And that's why they are less comprehensible for mere mortals. That is the face of the girl-artist I saw. It was unnerving. Later I thought a lot about that face and regretted that I didn't dare to speak to her....

And two years ago I saw her again at the seashore. Though, it was not easy to recognize her. As I mentioned, her face, arms, legs were covered in bruises and scratches. Some were very fresh, some were healing. Her face, if one looked at it from one side, was almost flat as if it had been drawn on paper, her wrists were tiny, like those of a child. Of course, her gaze had changed. Emptiness was no longer there, only wonder. To see it was even more unbearable.

Angie sat drawing portraits among other artists on the seafront. I ordered mine. While she was drawing, a fire was burning within me. Actually, that was not the first time I had felt that kind of fire within me during my stay in your wonderful but savage country. Maybe it was because my ancestors were born there.... But for me, all the pain from what I had seen and learned was as if it were concentrated in that girl. I didn't dare talk to her. In about forty minutes (I did all I could to delay the completion of the portrait – I took a bit of time to smoke and didn't sit still) she finished the job. I liked the portrait. I paid twice the sum she asked for it. But Angie gave me back the change. I stepped away a bit and started observing. I saw a fellow in sweat pants approach her, and Angie gave him the money. The fellow counted off a paltry sum of money and gave it back to her. She smiled gratefully and stood still again, watching the flow of vacationers. She worked with pleasure. I watched her till late night. In the light of street lamps, she looked like a translucent nocturnal butterfly.

Then she gathered her things and went toward the market stalls. There she bought some potato chips and coffee in a plastic cup and went somewhere deep into a cypress alley.

The fire was burning even worse. She was not supposed to be there! I felt that with every cell of my body. You do understand what I'm saying, don't you?

I was standing in the shade of an old wide-branching tree and was ready to stay there till morning if she (and it was very plausible) chose to sleep there on the bench. However, having eaten the chips, she headed toward the beach, where a bunch of vagrants had already fixed the fire. I hardly managed to catch up to her near the steps of the wooden fence.

I don't remember what I said....

Only much later did I understand that words meant for Angie as little as money did. She trusted her feelings. She smiled at me. At that moment I felt as if I had bathed in sunshine. I asked her to join me for dinner. From askance, it must have appeared quite wicked.... But Angie was removed from reality. When somebody stretched their hand with a piece of bread to her, she couldn't refuse it. As simple as that....

Back then I thought that, taking everything so literally, she must have had many unpleasant and maybe even dangerous moments.

...They wouldn't let us in to any more or less decent restaurant. Ragged jeans and a faded T-shirt were all she had to wear. That was all that belonged to her, except for a linen basket with paper and pastel pencils.

Then I took her to a twenty-four-hour supermarket, took everything that we could eat in the hotel room without cooking it. Thank God, times had changed, and I could take her to my room without any problems. I gave her a robe and showed her to the bathroom.

When she came out, I was surprised. She was a real beauty. I had first noticed it there, in the mountains. And now she appeared so radiant, with long reddish hair, and a fine, delicate face, so graceful in her every move. I was embarrassed, the way people are embarrassed in the presence of royal family members.

So that's how it was, how it all began....

I sat in the chair all night watching her sleep. I think that was the first time that she slept in a normal bed since our first meeting. I never let her go after that.

I don't know how romantic you are, or if you are able to understand me, but I felt that a star fell into my hands....

When, in the morning, I asked her what her name was, she uttered a strange word, some strange sound: "I-e-la-num"....

Back then I knew very little about her, but I understood that I had to take her away from there. Take her out, just like one takes ancient icons and antiquities out of the country. No, please don't think that I thought of her as of an expensive thing or just a beautiful woman. Trust me, I've seen both in my life....

It took me almost half a year to make her legal, buy her new documents and take her out of the country.

We moved from town to town. I did research work, which allowed me to move freely within the country. To the study of fifteenth century art I also added the theme of folklore in ancient Ukrainian embroidery, and because of that we could travel to the remotest corners of the country. In fact, I finished my work and had no concern for it anymore. All this time I was taking care of Angie. She finally started to talk and eat normally....

I have to make a confession here. One day, by coincidence, (it was at a hair salon in a small regional center) I saw you on TV. It was one of the numerous talk shows. The TV-set was in the middle of the room, and I cast glances at the screen involuntarily like the rest of the clients. I paid no attention until I saw Angie's photograph. I could hardly stay in my seat!

I didn't sleep that night.... Now I knew that Angie had run away from home, that she had you. But nothing else. Besides, I didn't dare to ask her more. My questions caused her such fits of despair that we had to resort to drugs. I dreamt about taking her out of the country as soon as possible and having her examined by the best psychiatrist whom I personally knew.

That night after the TV-show, one question haunted my mind: can I give her to you? It was a rhetorical question. I had an unambiguous answer to it. But I saw your eyes! And if earlier I thought you were a despot and a villain, now that impression was gone. I understood that something didn't work out. Something at a "higher" level, about which I should know nothing....

You'll be probably surprised, but I did find you. I wanted to see you. My decision was irrational and almost feminine. Since only women want to meet their rival to make sure that she is... younger and prettier. But I had a different purpose in mind: I wanted to make sure that I was doing the right thing.

We had a few days left before we were supposed to leave the country, and we spent them in the capital. Angie wouldn't leave the hotel room, and I was settling some matters. You probably want to know if I tried to find her parents. I did. And everything to my benefit there. Her mother was in a mental institution, her father had another wife and, judging by the TV programs, was immersed in political games. So, only you were left. And I decided to wait for you near the front door. Yes, I saw you.... You exited the building, went to your car, stood for a while, and lit a cigarette. I was absorbing your every move. Just imagine, had I approached you... Angie could have been with you an hour later. I hesitated just for a moment. And during that moment I realized: it's not worth it. Please don't think I'm saying this to justify my decision. No. If Angie could ever be happy with you, I would have backed off. But in your country, I've made a few odd observations: men always require a victim here. It has never made any sense to me! You have amazingly beautiful women, more so, they desire you and bow low before you, they try to stay in the shadows and please you, despite the fact that they get exhausted and suffer no less than you. You pass from your mother's hand to your fiancées' hand, continuing to be children.... I couldn't leave Angie in that world! I didn't want her to make excuses to you.... Not now, not ever....

...I will send you this letter, delete your e-mail address, and change mine immediately. When Angie comes back from the hospital, she will not remember that she ever wrote to you. I hope it was her last psychiatric examination....

I'll go get her in a few weeks. I know she'll sit in a chair on our balcony, and I'll roll her legs in an afghan, and she'll be gazing at the ocean.... And I'll be looking at her touching slender neck, feeling that my soul is at peace: I've found what I've always been missing in this frantic world.

And one last thing. This is the most difficult thing for me to write. But I must say it, and you must know it: *she doesn't love me....*

Good-bye!